AUSTIN BROWER

The Echo Machine

Thirteen months have passed since Amelia and Jesse received the threatening letter from former President Jason King, who vowed to continue his work on a time machine, a chilling reminder of their past...

First edition

Editing by Robin LeeAnn
Cover art by Jacob Calderon

This book was professionally typeset on Reedsy.
Find out more at reedsy.com

To my girlfriend, family, friends, and fans for their unwavering love and support.

"The past is never dead. It's not even past."

— William Faulkner

Contents

Foreword

In "The Echo Machine," Austin Brower takes us on a thrilling journey through the intricate world of time travel and its profound impact on the human heart. This captivating tale explores themes of loss, perseverance, and the enduring power of love in the face of seemingly insurmountable odds. Austin Brower masterfully weaves together elements of mystery, suspense, and science fiction, creating a narrative that will keep you on the edge of your seat until the very last page. Prepare to be transported to a world where the past and future collide, and where the choices we make today can have far-reaching consequences.

Preface

"The Echo Machine" began with a simple question: What if we could change the past? As I delved deeper into this concept, I became fascinated by the emotional complexities it presented. How would we grapple with the consequences of altering time? What would it mean to confront our deepest regrets and losses? This book is the result of that exploration, a journey into the lives of characters who are forced to confront these questions head-on. It is a story about love, loss, and the enduring power of hope, even in the face of the impossible.

Acknowledgments

I would like to express my sincere gratitude to the following people:

To my editor, Robin LeeAnn, for her invaluable feedback and guidance throughout this process.

To my cover artist and business partner, Jacob Calderon, for his insightful comments and unwavering support.

To my family and friends, for their patience and encouragement during the long hours of writing.

And finally, to the readers, for embarking on this journey with me. I hope this story resonates with you as much as it has with me.

Prologue

After the loss of Silas, Amelia and Jesse continued their work. They still greatly missed their friend and partner. Amelia is still recovering from the loss of her partner and future, and she sees him everywhere she goes. They expanded their company in Dallas and built several machines to help with the influx of companies wanting to use their product. Everything was working smoothly until they started delving into the secret file that Silas left behind: the "Future Project".

Introduction

For thirteen months, Amelia and Jesse have tried to move on, to bury the trauma of their past, and to focus on their work with time travel projects. The threatening letter from former President Jason King still hangs over them, a constant reminder of their conflict with him and the devastating loss of their partner, Silas. They witnessed Silas's death, yet the mysteries that continue to unfold make them question what they believe to be true.

When Amelia and Jesse begin to delve into Silas's old research, they uncover a project of immense potential—and danger. Silas's drawings of the Vale Machine and the cryptic "Future Project" hint at secrets that could redefine time travel itself. As they chase the truth, Amelia and Jesse must confront not only the enigma of Silas's possible survival but also the growing suspicion that they are not alone in their pursuit. The deeper they dig, the greater the risks they face, and the closer they get to understanding the true nature of the Echo Machine

1

Chapter One: Starting Over

Sitting at her desk, Amelia pours over her paperwork after paperwork, trying to search through pharmaceutical companies for her time travel project. The one currently in front of her was called DrugTopia, which she considered an interesting name. They were helping to fight Alzheimer's.

Jesse, her partner, walked into their office. "I didn't think we would get this busy, but I guess I should have thought better."

She barely looked up from her paperwork.

He pulled up a chair to her desk. "Which one is this one?"

"DrugTopia."

They continued to talk about the drug company and how they would make them a proposition about how they could benefit their company and the amount of money they could bring.

This had become their norm ever since they had received that threatening letter from former president Jason King—about how he would continue to work on his own time machine and how he would make sure they regret their actions. It had been a little over a year—thirteen months to be exact—since. They tried looking for Silas—their third partner who Jason had sent a photo of, one where their partner was hooked up to different hospital machines. They called every hospital in the surrounding area and even made a few trips, but nothing. They couldn't find him. The police also didn't report anything as if nothing had ever happened.

Just like Jason wanted.

They eventually gave up, assuming Jason was messing with them. They saw Silas die. They knew there was nothing left to search for. Devastated, they forced themselves back to work because that was where they felt closer to him. It also got their minds off him.

Later that afternoon, they looked over a few more documents before calling it a day. They ended up sitting in silence.

"Do you ever think about that day we got the letter?" Jesse asked, looking down at the ground. "Like why would Jason do that? I feel like there was a hidden agenda behind it."

Amelia looked up from the stack of paperwork still covering her desk, her brow furrowed. "I had the same feeling. But I looked at that photo over a hundred times. Studied it. Nothing leads me to believe he's still alive in a coma. It has to be fake, a last jab at us. I–I can't keep thinking about it as anything else. It's just going to break me more than it already has."

He nodded. "I know. A–and I'm sorry for bringing it up. It's just...it's just something that has been bothering me."

She set the paper she held down and leaned back. "I know... Trust me, I know. It bothers me every day too. But what can we do? We tried... And let's say he is alive, right? Why hasn't he reached out? And if he can't, we don't even know how to find him."

He numbly nodded.

"I'm not giving up on him, okay? But he's gone, Jesse. He

died, and it...and it hurts me every time I-I have to think about that."

They didn't speak any more about it and finished their work. It really was like a typical job: meetings, sales pitches, paperwork, more meetings, more paperwork, and time travel.

As the day ended, they grabbed their paperwork and put it all away in file cabinets. They also took home a few things to work on. Their noses had been so buried in paperwork all day that they didn't realize the rainstorm outside until they walked out of the office.

"It is coming down," Amelia said.

They said their goodbyes and took off to their vehicles. However, running didn't help them stay dry.

By the time she got into her vehicle, she was soaked. Moving her wet hair off her face, she started her car, shivered, and begged her car to warm up. It eventually warmed up just enough for her to drive home.

While driving home, she thought about changing her daily route as the spur of the moment, not really knowing why. She decided to drive by Silas's old apartment building, where she ended the lease and put his stuff in storage. Couldn't bring herself to sell his stuff and couldn't afford his place along with hers. Maybe driving by was a last-ditch effort to see if he was standing outside. Waiting for her.

She pulled up to the complex and sighed. It was exactly how it was when she canceled the lease.

Laughing at herself, she said, "How much of a fool are you? He isn't here..." She put the vehicle back in drive. As she started to drive away, a figure appeared a few feet in front of her, and she slammed her brakes.

The heavy rain didn't let her quite make out who was there.

She flipped her windshield wipers to a higher speed and realized it was a man. Silas.

"No... No, it can't be..."

But she couldn't convince herself it wasn't him.

She slowly opened her car door to get out and confirm her suspicion. Yet once she stood, he was gone. Whatever or whoever it was had disappeared.

"I must be losing my damn mind," she muttered. Getting back in the car, she wondered if it was him though. But if so, how did he get out here? How was he alive?

Someone slammed on their horn. Some douchebag in an overly large truck that was compensating for things. She flipped him the bird and drove off, heading home through the rain.

She turned on her music to drown out her thoughts. Yet she still couldn't shake the eerie feeling that lingered, the uncertainty of what she had just seen gnawing at her. The rain pounded on the roof of her car, mirroring the chaotic storm of emotions inside her. She just couldn't dismiss the possibility that what she saw was real.

But it defied all logic and reason.

As she pulled into her driveway, she couldn't help but replay the brief encounter in her mind. Silas—or someone who looked exactly like him—stood there in the rain. Only to vanish into thin air. It was a perplexing enigma indeed.

She hurried to her door, unlocked it, and rushed inside to her new companion, Lucy. Lucy was her bundle of joy. She didn't know what kind of dog Lucy was, just a mixed breed of brown and white. She had found her on the streets a few months ago, and while Lucy seemed like an adult dog, she still acted like a puppy. Not the sharpest tool in the shed. But she didn't care. Lucy's unwavering loyalty and sweet nature had won her heart.

"Hello, my baby," she said with a slight baby voice. She crouched to the dog's height as Lucy jumped on her, licking her face. "Were you a good girl today? Did the thunder scare you? Of course, it didn't. You're the strongest girl ever."

Amelia had often wondered about Lucy's past. How she ended up on the streets. What adventures—including ones with thunderstorms—she might have had before becoming a part of her life. Despite her mysterious origins, Lucy had seamlessly integrated into her daily routine.

Amelia continued to shower Lucy with affectionate words as the dog eagerly showered her with affectionate licks. To her, Lucy was not just a pet but a cherished friend who had helped fill the void left by Silas.

After their heartwarming reunion, Amelia wasted no time in attending to her own needs. Her drenched clothes found their way into the washing machine, and she reveled in the warmth of a thick fluffy towel around her shivering body. She also let her paperwork she had taken home dry out on the kitchen countertops, hoping they would still be readable in the morning.

Her cozy home, accompanied by the soothing, beating rain outside, created a comforting sanctuary. She went ahead and poured herself a glass of red wine, which she typically drank while ending her day.

She sat on the couch while Lucy hopped up right next to her, did a few spins, rested her head on her lap, and let out a long sigh as if she had just taken on the world. She pet her head while the rhythm of rain hitting the roof synced with Lucy's tail tapping away on the armrest.

Amelia turned on the television and selected her and Silas's favorite show, *South Park*. It was crude humor, but they both loved it. She set her glass down, grabbed her phone off the side table, and texted Jesse to let him know she was home safe and apologized that it took a bit longer than normal. He ended up replying right away, letting her know the same. He also informed her that Sandra would like to know if she would come over for dinner tomorrow night. She agreed. She had gotten much closer with his family over the last year; his family always ensured she had people around.

As she watched their show throughout the night, her mind drifted back to Silas and the disappearing figure. She eventually concluded that it had to be her imagination playing tricks on her. Silas was gone, and the past was a chapter she couldn't rewrite.

2

Chapter Two: Unveiled

Amelia woke drenched from her nightmares—from recurring visions of Silas being shot over and over and over again. She lay there with her eyes shut, trying to forget what she had dreamed. Not that she wasn't used to it in some aspects. She had been dreaming of this almost every night since they got back from the bread factory incident.

Her bed moved, and a wet force pressed slid up her face. This familiar sensation was not pleasant, but she knew who it was. Lucy was trying to help her again. Though between the nightmares and Lucy's tongue, she didn't even need an alarm clock anymore.

First on the agenda was a visit to the great outdoors. Lucy's wagging tail and almost tangible enthusiasm bounded toward the back door, ready to embark on her morning mission.

She slowly got up, stretching as Lucy came running back. Lucy bounced on and off the bed, excited to go outside. She walked to the back door and saw all the mud.

"Now, Lucy," she said even though Lucy didn't understand her words. "Now, don't go out playing in the mud. Pee and then come back. No mud."

Lucy looked at her and tilted her head as if confused by the allegations of why she would assume one would go play in the mud. Amelia sighed, patted her on the head, and swung the door open. She bolted outside, looking for any enemy squirrels trying to make fun of her today. She stayed alert even as she peed to make sure the backyard was well protected under any circumstances.

Amelia started the coffee maker. While she waited for that to heat up, she stood in the doorway, watching Lucy. The dog was out back, sniffing around an old trail of invading animals that had explored her backyard while she was inside. She soon found a particular smell and dug.

"Lucy! No! What did I say? Get back in here."

She looked up at her, confused why she was interrupting her digging. She then bounded toward the house like a bull in a China shop.

Amelia jumped out of the doorway as she ran through. While she poured her food, she ran a few quick laps around the kitchen and living room before calming down in time for Amelia to set her bowl on the floor. Amelia made herself a small breakfast and checked her emails while she ate.

Once she finished her breakfast, she checked over the papers that she had left out to dry due to the rain. In one of the stacks, she stopped at a page that stood out. Silas's intricate drawings of The Vale Machine and different variations of it. She sat there, admiring and studying the details. The variations sparked her curiosity.

She grabbed Silas's old laptop that she had kept, powered it on, and scrolled through the numerous files until she found what she was looking for—the Future Project. As she scrolled through page after page of formulas, and drawings, and complex diagrams, she wondered what he could have been working on that was so important that he had to bring it back from the future.

She scanned through the file as she and Jesse had done before plenty of time. The screen filled with the same confusing schematics and complexities. The more she studied it, the more lost and confusing it became. She put the laptop in her bag and decided to discuss it with Jesse again later.

She got dressed and let Lucy out to pee one last time. After she let Lucy in, she grabbed her bag. As she opened the front door to leave, she turned back and said, "I will be back at lunch to let you out again. Please don't destroy anything." She kissed her head.

She then locked the door behind her.

The drive to work was a familiar routine; she knew it like the back of her hand. However, today felt different. Thoughts of yesterday and the Future Project circled her brain, leaving lingering questions. She couldn't help but wonder what connection they might have to Silas.

When she pulled up to the office, the company had a bustling energy around it. Every worker and security personnel—that they hired from a private contracting company they had vetted ever since the Control team—seemed to be on a mission and on top of their job. This gave her a contact high, pushing the gnawing questions out of her mind for the moment.

As she walked into her and Jesse's shared office space, she didn't see him anywhere. Strange. He usually was the first one there.

She figured he must be in one of the other offices, working on a project. With a determined resolve, she put the file and questions to the side until she could discuss them with him later. At her desk, she sat and focused on the tasks at hand, immersing herself in the daily grind of time travel, negotiations, and pharmaceutical companies.

But like a worm eating into an apple, thoughts and questions of Silas and his project inched into the core of her mind. As she shifted through her dried paperwork from the rain, she noticed that several documents had been ruined. She decided to just reprint the entire batch. As she was getting ready to reprint the destroyed collection, in came Jesse with coffee and a smile.

"Good morning." He handed her a cup of coffee. "Ruined paperwork too?"

She took a sip and nodded.

He set his stuff down on his nearby desk. "How is your day going?"

She mustered a smile. "Pretty good." However, she found herself contemplating whether to share the strange experience she had last night outside Silas's former apartment now. She knew Jesse knew her too well to just accept that mustered smile. She would have to bring it up eventually.

He got up to leave to check on one of the machines. As he was heading toward the door, she spoke.

"Hey, Jesse. I need to tell you something, but don't think I've lost my mind."

He closed the door, turned around, and sat.

She sighed before recounting her visit to Silas's old apartment and her surreal encounter in the pouring rain. She couldn't help but mention how she believed she had seen him or someone resembling him. Jesse listened attentively and didn't say anything. After she finished, he leaned back in his chair, and his expression became contemplative.

"I know what you are talking about," he said. "I have seen him too. Or…at least I think I have."

She stared at him, wondering if he was just telling her that. Or meant it like he missed Silas too. Was he joking? Or did he have a better explanation? "What do you mean?"

Jesse met her gaze. "I thought it was just my imagination, but there have been these moments when I swear I saw him. Like a few weeks ago when I had gone to the park with my family. In the distance, I spotted a figure that looked just like him. I rushed toward him, but he ducked behind a tree. The moment I had reached the tree, he had vanished. I don't know. Maybe we are both losing our minds. Or perhaps it is him. Maybe Jason wasn't lying, and he is alive."

Both surprise and intrigue filled Amelia. She had thought her encounter was a product of her imagination, but now, hearing his similar experience, doubt crept in.

Her voice was tinged with a mixture of hope and skepticism. "You…you've seen him too?"

He nodded solemnly. "I know it sounds wild, but yes. I've had a few instances where I thought I saw him, but usually, I would dismiss it as wishful thinking or my mind playing tricks on me. But after hearing your story, I can't ignore the possibility. Or, as I said, we are both out of our minds." He laughed.

She leaned forward, her curiosity growing. "What did you see? Tell me more about it."

He recounted his experiences, describing how each time he had spotted the figure resembling Silas at a distance. Only for the person to vanish into thin air. As if he had never existed at all. The memories were still vivid, and he couldn't shake the feeling that there was more to it.

Amelia listened intently. Once he finished, she sat back and sipped her coffee. "I don't know, Jesse. This is so weird that we are both experiencing them, but honestly...I can't do this. I can't keep living like he's alive. We both saw him die. We both probably just want to see him when he isn't there. I just don't want to torture myself with the idea he is alive when he isn't."

He nodded. "I know this is hard on me, and I can't even begin to imagine how hard it is on you, Amelia. Truly. If I lost Sandra and watched her...watched her..." He took a deep breath to steady himself. "Well, you know. My life would be a mess, and I wouldn't want to think about the possibility of her being alive."

She looked down at her desk.

"Let's just focus on the work at hand. Maybe we can reach out to Scarlet and see if she has any updates about Jason."

Amelia nodded. "Since I have you for a moment, could you look over the file Silas created one more time with me? I've been looking over the drawings he did, but I just can't make sense of what it means or why he would do this."

He smiled and pulled up a chair next to her. "Of course."

They looked over the file for a moment.

"You know, I never really looked at this in great detail with everything that was going on before and just didn't put two and two together. What started your interest in looking into them?"

She leaned forward, her face filled with curiosity. She told him about how she was skimming through her paperwork that had finally dried from the rainstorm the prior day and had found a stack of his drawings that must have slipped in. "We already have the calculations and science behind time travel. What else would he be so keen on bringing back from the future?"

Holding one of the drawings, he said, "You might be onto something. Maybe we should put some time aside and look into this. Maybe we missed something. Or maybe it's just slight modifications." He pulled out his phone and looked at his calendar. "Let's see... We have a meeting today, but tomorrow we have some free time, so we can look more into this then."

"Oh, good. That sounds like a plan, Jesse. Let's do that."

He added it to his calendar, got up, and left to work on a few things before their meeting.

She sat there, pondering where this path might lead them and what it could all mean. She pulled up her calendar on her computer and saw she had two trips scheduled for today—one for a cancer research team and another involving a hair loss prevention medication.

The morning carried on until it was time to meet up with the research team. She left her office and walked down the hall, where she saw them signing into the front desk.

"Hello, and welcome," she said. "Thank you for joining us today. If you follow me, I'll go ahead and get you set up."

They followed her to machine room two, where there was a Vale Machine and a few tables with chairs. She had them sit as she went over the typical speech, reminding them of the formalities of time travel. With that, a technician walked in, and she introduced him as their "traveling agent." He had been given the name and address of where he would be traveling to, the research team let both her and him know where the documentation, from the course of thirty years, would be when he arrived.

Once everything was ready to go, the agent got into the bed, and Amelia hooked him up.

"You ready?" she asked.

He nodded.

She counted down from five, and then he was out.

"What now?" one of the research members asked.

"We wait. Should just be a few minutes."

She explained the different machine mechanics and briefly how it worked. They asked questions about the machine and where they got the name Vale from. She had become used to this question, and discussing Silas Vale's namesake had gotten easier.

To her benefit, the travel agent woke up. Perfect timing. She unhooked him from the machine.

"All right," she said. "He will take it from here and answer your questions. Thank you for coming by." She then walked out of the room and back toward her office, where she logged the numbers and information from the travel.

She found herself glancing at the clock more often than usual, eagerly anticipating tomorrow. She couldn't wait to decipher the file alongside Jesse. She knew there might be nothing to it, but curiosity still clawed at her.

3

Third Chapter: Known in the Unknown

The following day, Jesse sat at a long table next to the door in the room with the original time machine. He heard Amelia walk in with a pep in her step, looked up from his notes, and grinned. "You brought coffee and donuts! My hero!"

She smiled, placing the coffee and donuts on the table before him. "Well, I figured we deserved something sweet, and who doesn't like to start with donuts and coffee?" She sat across from him as he opened the small box and snagged a donut.

They sat in silence for a moment, eating their breakfast and drinking their coffee. The mystery behind Silas's artwork and notes lingered between them.

"I'm glad we have this because as much as I love my job, I am excited to figure out this new puzzle," Amelia said, pulling out Silas's laptop from her bag.

Jesse nodded, finishing his last donut.

He grabbed Silas's computer and opened the Future Project file. She flipped through the notes and drawings as he printed out the documents and carried the laptop to the side of the room next to the machine. There, he sat at a desk with multiple monitors made for monitoring the travel agents and the coding for the machine. She walked over to the printer, grabbed the printed documents, and pulled up a chair next to him. She set the documents and drawings next to the laptop and looked up to see that he had hooked up the laptop to the monitors.

"So, where should we even start?" she asked.

"I don't know. Honestly, I guess let's start by scanning through the files to see if we can understand anything."

They sat there, meticulously scanning every file. Each time they thought they got close, they ran the code, but it kept failing. So, they would go back and try again. They even went back to the beginning and redid a few steps, experimenting with different mathematical approaches to get a better result. Yet the code still failed.

Amelia and Jesse were sucked into their work, their minds immersed in the intricate codes and calculations. The room filled with the soft hum of computer fans and the click–clack of keyboards. They were hunched over the computer and papers while bouncing ideas off each other for so long that they hadn't even realized that hours had passed. The sunlight through the small window gradually shifted, casting long shadows across the room. Yet they continued to dive deeper. The room's air grew thick with a sense of purpose and the thrill of discovery.

They eventually decided to take a small lunch break, leaving a few programs to run tests in their absence. Amelia went home to take care of Lucy, and Jesse went to surprise his daughter at school for lunch. She arrived back at the office first and walked back into the room they had blocked off from the rest of the building. The programs were still running. Jesse walked in a few minutes later, sat, and talked about his lunch date, where he had gotten burgers with his daughter.

After he caught her up on his date, she pulled up the test screen. It had failed again.

Out of frustration, they decided to take a break from working in front of the computers and took a look at the drawings and diagrams they had printed out. The diagrams were of The Vale Machine, but as they looked more into it, the pieces in the drawings had a few different parts. They decided to start by taking the machine apart.

They meticulously disassembled the plating and examined the guts of the machine. Their heads shifted from the papers to the wires and nobs and back to the papers. They started dissecting the parts that had not been in the diagrams. Jesse ran and grabbed more tools and supplies from their parts room. Beads of sweat rolled down their faces as they shifted parts, replaced wires, and removed unnecessary items. Once they finished one section, they moved on to the next, and to the next, and so on.

As Amelia lay under the machine, rewiring it like a mechanic, she hoped the changes they were making to the machine would help with the failing code. Maybe—just maybe—this was what was needed.

"Done," Jesse said as he stepped back, wiping the sweat from his brow.

"I think we should just double-check everything one more time," she said, rolling out from under the machine.

They made one last walk, checking over everything. Afterward, he looked at the time and had the brilliant idea to order pizza since they might be there for a bit longer. He put in the order and told his wife that he wouldn't be home for dinner but wouldn't be too late. Amelia left to let Lucy out and feed her, and on her way back, she grabbed the pizza and a large bottle of orange soda.

When she arrived back at the office, Jesse sat at the desk once more, looking through the computer and trying different tests. "Perfect timing for a break," he said, looking up toward the smell of pizza.

He joined her at the table, and they ate, exhausted and nearly brain dead from the number of numbers, the papers, the files, and the diagrams. She talked about how Lucy wanted to come along and how she had promised she could tag along another time.

Once they finished their dinner, they went back to work. They put together one last group of functions and programs for the computers to run with the machine's new changes. An hour passed, and they figured they decided to change the function of a few codes. She finished up the rest of the functions while he cleaned up their mess and organized the papers that had somehow been strewn along the floor.

Amelia clicked to run the program. "Alrighty. That should be good while we head home."

He grabbed the bag of trash. "Awesome. Let's get out of this room and enjoy an hour or two of daylight before the sun sets."

They both bid farewell to their staff and to each other and headed to their respective homes.

Amelia was greeted by Lucy as if she had been gone for weeks or months. She decided it would be nice to take her for a walk in the park and get a change of scenery. Plus, she hadn't taken her on a walk in a good while. She grabbed Lucy's leash and changed into something a bit more comfortable, and off they went. As she walked Lucy—or more like as Lucy walked Amelia—she shut off her brain, deciding to just enjoy the evening. Lucy went this way and that, smelling new and old smells.

They strolled down to the neighborhood park that was only a few blocks away. The sun was low but still beaming. Smelling the scents of her friends and new dogs, Lucy pulled at her leash harder as they got closer to the park. Amelia laughed at her excitement, and they jogged to the dog park. As they strolled up to the gate, Lucy whined, her tail swinging like a baseball bat.

The sounds of the neighborhood filled the air—dogs barking and playing in the dog park, kids screaming as they played on the nearby jungle gym. A reminder of the simple pleasures. Amelia smiled, taking it all in and watching Lucy run around to greet the other dogs. She sat on a bench, keeping an eye on her little horse galloping around the park. As the sun shined down on her, she realized she should've brought her sunglasses.

She lifted her hand to block out the sun and to keep an eye on her baby while she played with the other dogs, but a figure caught her eye across the park on the other side of the street. A man stood there, staring at her. Blood soaked his shirt. Her breathing quickened as her eyes held the man's gaze.

"Silas," she whispered.

She stood and started walking toward the man, keeping her eyes locked on him. She closed the dog park gate behind her, and her walk turned into a run. Then a sprint. The man simply stood there.

The closer she got, the clearer he became. His arms and face were purple and bruised, and his eyes were sunken in and bloodshot.

"Silas!" she yelled.

But he didn't move. He didn't come toward her.

She continued to run. At the edge of the park, she stepped off the sidewalk, and a horn blared. She looked left. A bus sped toward her. She jumped back as it tried to slow down, and she fell onto her back—nearly getting hit. The bus sped back up after the driver saw she was out of the road. When it passed, her view cleared, but Silas was gone.

Yet in his place was a homeless man with a sign that said he was looking for work.

She shook her head. There was no way her eyes could have played a trick like that. Her mind scrambling, she got up and went to the man.

"Excuse me," she said, his eyes turning to her. "Did you see someone else just standing here?"

He shook his head. "No one here but me."

Sighing, she turned around and noticed that all the other dog parents had watched it all go down. They must've thought she had lost her mind.

Embarrassed and irritated, she walked back over to the dog park, called for Lucy, leashed her, and headed back home.

Her heart raced, and her mind churned with a whirlwind of emotions. She couldn't shake the image of the bloody man standing across the street. A part of her conceded that maybe she did need help.

When they arrived back home, she tried to dismiss the whole thing.

She slammed down four fingers deep of tequila. The warmth and sting offered some solace. She sighed and looked down at Lucy sitting next to her bowl. "All right. All right. I'll give you a snack, but you already ate your dinner." She poured some food into the bowl, which was wolfed down.

Amelia reached into her cabinet, grabbed a pack of cookies, and sat on the couch. As she ate cookies and down more glasses of tequila, she sat in silence. Now warm and slightly dizzy, she got up, grabbed a bottle of tequila, poured herself another glass, and set the cookies on the counter and out of Lucy's line of vision. With her glass, she drew herself a bath with some Epsom salt and vanilla oil and stepped into the water, one foot at a time to get used to the heat. After a moment, she set her glass and phone to the side, submerged herself, and closed her eyes, allowing the oils and salt to do their work.

After a few minutes, she decided to look on her social media. Pictures of Jesse and his daughter at the school cafeteria appeared. They brought a smile to her face. She continued to scroll until she received a notification from Scarlet on their secure messaging app. She opened it.

It was Scarlet just checking in.

Scarlet had been keeping in touch with Amelia and Jesse over the past year, also keeping them updated on the search for Jason. But so far, she had little to no luck. He had gone off the radar after quitting his presidential term, which shocked everyone except the few who knew him.

They texted back and forth for a while. Amelia sent photos of Lucy, and Scarlet updated her on her still fruitless search for her father.

As she exchanged messages, her thoughts kept returning to the possible Silas sightings, especially the one from earlier. She leaned back in the tub, closing her eyes and trying to clear her mind.

"It couldn't have been him," she whispered to herself.

But it kept gnawing at her. The vividness... It couldn't have been a hallucination... Or could it?

She decided to inform Scarlet of the incidents, but Scarlet didn't think she was losing her mind. Just her brain playing tricks on her. Scarlet also reminded her that she has people almost everywhere, and that if there is something, she will hear about it.

She set her phone down on the side of the tub and noticed that Lucy had snuck in and curled up on the tile floor. Her big brown eyes were shut, and her heavy breathing signified that she was sleeping. She reached down and scratched Lucy's head.

She got out of the bath, dried off, slipped into one of Silas's hoodies and boxers, and crawled into bed. For a few hours, she lay there, staring at the ceiling and watching the fan spin round and round. As the effects of the liquor wore off, she rolled over and looked at the clock, which showed one a.m. She sighed. She then rolled onto her stomach to attempt to sleep. After some more tossing and turning, she realized she couldn't.

She got up, and so did Lucy.

"Let's go, missy," she told the dog. "We are going to the office."

4

The Fourth Chapter: Uncharted Threads

Jesse arrived at the facility the next morning and greeted everyone as usual. However, when he opened the door to the room with the original time machine, he found Amelia slouched over one of the computers, softly snoring. Lucy was sleeping on her back nearby. Chuckling to himself, he set the coffee he had brought for her down, cleared his throat, and gently woke her up.

"Huh? What?" she mumbled half awake, startled.

He pushed the coffee toward her. "Couldn't sleep?"

She shook her head and took a few gulps of the coffee before explaining her recent Silas incident.

"I'm so sorry it happened again. I know it is strange and frustrating to see him and then him not being there." He settled into a nearby chair and sipped his coffee. "Any luck last night?" he asked, pointing toward the machine.

She shook her head. "The code is still running from when we left yesterday."

They sat in silence for a while, contemplating their options and wondering why this endeavor had proved to be so challenging.

"I could understand if we were starting from scratch, but we aren't. We already have the machine built. We just modified it."

After a few minutes to allow her to wake up, they decided to set aside their current project for the morning for a video conference scheduled with a lab out in the UK. She needed to take care of a few things—like to take Lucy home and to change—and he said he would prepare the conference room for the meeting. About an hour later, she returned to the facility. She entered the conference room with her folders filled with proposals and pricing options for their services.

The scheduled time arrived, and they joined the video call. They had a marketing and sales team, but most of the time, the major companies wanted to hear from Amelia and Jesse, so these calls had become second nature. He provided the humor and care while she provided the charm and determination. Together, they always won the sale.

After wrapping up the successful conference call, they felt a sense of accomplishment. They handed off the paperwork to the next team, who would prep and schedule everything out.

As they walked down to their office, Amelia couldn't help but smile. "You know, I never get tired of these. Even though they are super boring, with us working together, it makes my job so much easier."

He laughed. "Well, we make a great team. And your determination and sharp negotiation skills are very impressive."

She nodded. "We do complement each other well. That's for sure."

Almost back at their office, she decided to check on the

machine room for any updates first. As she approached it alone, a tapping noise echoed down the hallway. It sounded like water dropping in a cave. She wondered if there was a leak, trying to rationalize it. However, the tapping only grew louder as she neared the room.

She swung the door open, and the tapping continued. She walked in, searching for the noise. Then it hit her. The tapping was coming from the machine.

"This is new," she said. She backed out toward the door, and her voice dropped to a whisper. "It's working…"

She ran out of the room and down the hall, dodging colleagues and nearly missing their office.

At his desk, Jesse looked up at a breathless Amelia. "Yes?"

She held up a finger. As soon as she caught her breath, she said, "It's alive. Or working."

He sat up. "What do you mean?"

She motioned for him to follow. "Hurry!" And took off running again.

He followed, and as they got closer, the tapping echo surrounded him. They both entered the room, and the machine's hum filled the air but so did the tapping. They walked up to the machine and stood in awe. She could hardly contain her excitement.

After a few minutes, Jesse walked over to the computers and looked through the programs. "It's all good. Better than good. It's…excellent, and the machine is running at one hundred percent."

She walked over and verified for herself.

"Why is it making that noise though?"

She shrugged. "Maybe it is talking to us. Or maybe it just does that."

He nodded. "We need to document this. It could be a breakthrough."

They continued to photograph, videotape, and write down everything about it and compared it to the original machine.

Yet a fact bugged her. "Wait. What does it do exactly?"

Jesse looked over. "Honestly, I don't know. I don't remember if Silas even said anything about it."

She looked at the machine for a good minute before a name popped into her head. "I guess there's one way to find out, right?" She then turned around and looked at him. "Its name is Echo. The Echo Machine."

He stared at the machine and pondered the name. "The Echo Machine... It's fitting. I like it, but we still don't know what it does or what it's for." He turned his head and looked over at her, who had an enthusiastic grin on her face.

"Well, I guess there is one way to find out. Let's see what she does."

He smiled. "I like the way you think. But we must be cautious. It's unfamiliar territory. Let's run some diagnostics first. Observe its behaviors."

She agreed, and they ran diagnostic tests to see what kind of reaction they would get from it. As the tests ran, they analyzed the codes generated from the machine. He worked on the machine's controls while she operated the computing system.

"Ready?" she asked.

"Yes."

She entered the code, selected the configuration options, ensured the backup power options were activated, and clicked the Run button. The machine hummed, the sound growing in intensity along with the tapping. The tapping sped up, creating a stronger echoing effect, and the machine's lights rapidly blinked. A loud thud followed. Then silence.

Jesse hurried back to the control area. "So...?" he anxiously asked as he approached her.

"Nothing wrong yet. Waiting for the response."

They sat there, eyes glued to the computers. The room was silent as they held their breaths. After fifteen minutes, which felt like hours to them, information filled the screens with numbers, dates, times, and longitudes and latitudes coordinates.

Amelia pulled up a map and entered in the coordinates. "Weird."

"What?" Jesse replied, looking from her to the screen and then back at her.

Her face was scrunched. "This doesn't make sense."

"What does?"

"It...it ran the diagnostic test, and the results show today's date and time, but when it comes to the location, the coordinates don't match anywhere on the map. I entered the right coordinates. I made sure of it. But the ones that came back are...different."

"That doesn't make sense. Why would it do that?"

"I don't know. Maybe it's broken? What if we try it again with a rat or a guinea pig or something?"

They both agreed. Jesse ran to the lab and borrowed one of their guinea pigs. He hooked it up to the machine, and they ran the test again. The noises and lights reappeared. Then nothing. The guinea pig was simply asleep. They looked at each other and then over at the computer. Waiting. It took about the same amount of time, but they soon received the same coordinates and time. Yet the guinea pig was still under the machine.

"Where could it be then?" he asked.

"I don't know," Amelia replied.

"What should the coordinates be?"

"They should be this." She pointed at the map, which read 32° 51' 40.0" N 96° 39' 38.4" W.

"And the ones the computer is reading off are different?"

"Yeah. These are the computer ones." She pointed at the computer, which read 32° 51' 40.0" N3125 96° 39' 38.4" W3125.

"What could the numbers after the *N* and *W* mean?"

She sat there, pinching the bridge of her nose. "I don't know. I've never seen this before."

They decided to go ahead and clear their schedules for the next couple of days, passing their tasks off to some trusted colleagues. They then sat in that machine room, trying to figure out what the issue was while keeping an eye on the guinea pig throughout the night. Amelia agreed to stay till one a.m. Jesse came in and took over then, so she could go home and sleep for a few hours. When she came back that next morning, the guinea pig was still asleep, and he didn't have anything to update her on.

They continued to try various combinations of numbers, but the numbers after the *N* and *W* remained unexplained.

"Maybe it's a code or a cipher," he suggested. "Like a puzzle we need to solve."

She gazed off into the distance. "Maybe... Maybe it could be. It wouldn't hurt to dig into that. Let's see if the numbers match anything in the notes."

They spent that morning scouring through Silas's notes, searching for any reference to these odd coordinates. Nothing for the additional numbers. However, they found descriptions of other places—other worlds—that left them confused.

"Why would there be notations of different worlds?"

They continued scanning the paperwork and checking in on the computers when a squeak called out from behind them. They turned around. Their guinea pig was awake, squeaking at them.

"He is probably just upset and confused," Jesse said as he walked over and picked the guinea pig up. "Ouch!" He jolted back, holding his finger. "What the hell?!"

The guinea pig dropped to the ground with a soft thud and scurried away, squealing in anger.

"What was its problem?" she asked.

A small amount of blood rolled down his finger. She got up and walked over to the wall where they kept a first aid kit. She grabbed some antibiotic cream and a Band-Aid for Jesse. After she applied the cream and bandaged his finger, he thanked her.

They looked at the machine, still confused. Yet curiosity grew like cancer inside of Amelia.

"What if I go in?" she suggested. "The guinea pig survived."

He looked over at her with concern. "No, Amelia. It worked for the pig, but we don't know where it goes or what it does."

She sighed. "I know, but we aren't getting anywhere with all of these papers." She lifted a stack of papers, waving them. "I won't let you do it, Jesse. You have a wife and daughter and a future with them. Maybe this is my future. Silas left this for us, but I am the one to take the risk. Let me have this, Jesse. Please."

He hesitated but then sighed. "I just—"

"No. I *want* to do this, Jesse. If you won't help, then I'll find someone else."

He hugged her. "I know. I know. But let's go get lunch first before we do anything."

She smiled and nodded.

They left their paperwork and notes where they were, walked out of the room, and locked it behind them, ensuring no one would tamper with the machine by accident while they were at lunch. As they left the facility, they informed one of their colleagues that a guinea pig was on the loose. They decided on curry and enjoyed a beer as well as a celebration—and as a pre-celebration for when she successfully did whatever the machine did and came back alive.

When they finished up lunch, they headed back to the facility, full and in better spirits. They started up the machine again, entering in the coordinates as they did before. She lay on the bed as he hooked her up with wires and the IV. As he was connecting everything, he noticed she had a smile filled with comfort and excitement.

He smiled back and headed back over to the computers. "Are you ready?"

She turned her head to face him and laughed. "I'm ready. Let's do this."

He filled out the needed information and hit the Enter button to run the machine. The noises started up once again. The lights blinked as the sounds grew louder and louder, and then nothing. Silence.

She was out.

5

The Fifth Chapter: E-3125

A burning feeling overtook Amelia's lungs—as if a liquid was filling them—and she coughed. The smell of burning plastic, wood, and flesh surrounded her. She slowly opened her eyes, but the air stung them.

Smoke was everywhere. She climbed to her feet, lifted her shirt over her nose to breathe, and cracked her eyes open. Thick smoke lay everywhere. She extended one of her hands and slowly searched, tripping over something hard. Her hands felt the ground and encountered a soft and crispy material. She got her face close to it. A burnt body.

She jumped back and fell onto her butt. "Oh my god…" she muttered.

Slowly, she got to her feet again and pushed through the smoke like she was moving curtains out of the way to clear her sight. She watched her step as best as she could, stepping over smoldering wood and other objects she could not make out.

When she made it out of the pool of smoke, she fell to her hands and knees on the dirt. Her lungs grasped for fresh air.

Coughing. Her eyes were bloodshot, and spit dribbled off her lip. She wiped her eyes, squinting around. She then sat back on her heels, stunned.

"What the hell?"

Buildings had been burnt down like a child playing with building blocks and knocking them all down while pretending they were a giant. Rubble had been spewed everywhere. She got to her feet, jaw gapped, and stumbled down the street.

She turned a corner and saw a ripped poster that made her stop. She could barely make out what it said. *Emperor Jason King.* Below the words was a photo of him. This time, he had a salt-and-pepper beard, but she knew that smug face anywhere.

Her mind raced as she tried to piece the grim scenery around her together. "Is...is this the future? Another world?"

As she looked around, she recognized what the rubble had been. This was her facility. The same one she had been at moments ago.

She cautiously walked down the street, exploring the area. Trying to gain some bearings. The once familiar streets were now a haunting wasteland. A debris-laden city. The quiet, eerie silence was only broken by the occasional distant rumble from parts of buildings giving way or thuds from falling debris. A portion of the fifth floor wall had fallen to the ground, cracking the sidewalk and sending rubble in all directions.

She couldn't quite shake the feeling of isolation.

As she continued down the street, searching for life, terror gripped her. The further she journeyed, the less likely it seemed that she would find anyone. The destruction itself was overwhelming. Thoughts, concerning Jesse and his family and Silas, raced through her mind.

She crept inside the next building, taking great care to be

as quiet as possible. She searched for a bathroom, which she found, but the door was missing its top half. Bullet-sized holes covered the rest of it. It loudly creaked as it slowly opened. She froze. But there was no response.

Inside, she found a broken, dusty mirror. She wiped the grime, and her eyes widened at her reflection. It was her face and body, but she had red hair, bright blue eyes, and a scar along her cheek. She raised her hands, lightly touching the raised white skin. Her fingers combed through the strands of red hair. Her mind raced with questions.

It was as if she had stepped into an alternate version of herself.

She tried turning on the faucet, but no water came out. "Damn it!" She sighed and left the restroom.

Uncertainty weighed on her as she continued her exploration. The cityscape around her seemed both familiar and alien with shattered buildings and abandoned vehicles lining the streets. She couldn't shake the sensation that she had entered a dystopian nightmare.

After several hours of aimless wandering, she found herself standing outside Silas's apartment building. Her gaze drifted up toward the upper floors, which were now reduced to rubble. A deep sense of dread filled her.

"What has happened?" she muttered.

With a heavy heart, she entered the abandoned building and ascended the stairs to Silas's floor. Silently, she made her way down the dimly lit hallway. The door was ajar—as if it had been left open for her.

It appeared as though no one had lived there for quite some time. Only subtle changes had occurred. She ventured into the bedroom, where her eyes fell upon a framed photograph on the side table. She picked it up and carefully wiped away the dust that had gathered on its surface.

The photograph depicted Silas and herself on their wedding day, a moment of pure happiness forever captured in time. In the image, she wore a white wedding dress that faded into a pink and purple floral pattern at the hem. Around her neck, a necklace with a light purple sapphire shaped like a tulip adorned her. Silas was dressed in a black tuxedo with a dark floral tie and a matching vest. Both wore radiant smiles as he kissed her cheek.

A few tears streamed down her cheeks as she held the picture close to her heart.

She removed the photograph from its frame and noticed the writing on the back. A poignant message from Silas, a vow of eternal love that tugged at her heartstrings. A bittersweet reminder of the love she once had. Overwhelmed by the beauty of that moment and the pain of her current reality, she couldn't hold back her tears.

She sat on the edge of her bed, clutching the photograph. Eventually, she slid it into her pocket. Next to a phone. Her heart quickened with hope. She pulled it out and noticed that it had a satellite connection. A glimmer of anticipation lit up her eyes.

Leaving the apartment behind, she ran toward the stairs, determined to reach higher ground for a stronger signal. She pushed open the door to the top floor, revealing a view of the sky through the demolished ceiling. With the phone in her trembling hand, she watched as the signal grew stronger.

Her heart pounded. She scrolled through the contacts on the phone, her fingers hovering over Silas's name. Shivers ran down her spine. She wondered if it could be real. If he was alive here. After a few moments of internal struggle, she forced herself to call.

The phone rang, and her anticipation grew.

"Hello? Amelia? Are you okay?" a voice came over the phone.

She sank to her knees, tears streaming down her face. She struggled to catch her breath. "Silas?" she asked, her voice trembling.

"Yes? Amelia, where did you go? You said you would be back hours ago."

Her heart swelled. It was him. The man she was going to marry before he was taken from her. On the other end of the line. Alive and well. A miracle. She couldn't believe her ears. She choked back tears and struggled to speak as her voice quivered.

But this wasn't *her* Silas. *Her* Silas was somewhere hurt with the former president or dead. *This* Silas was married to the Amelia whose life she had taken over. She had to act like that Amelia.

"Hello?" he asked on the other line.

"Yes? Sorry," she responded, trying to hold back her tears. "The signal is bad. I got lost at the old facility, and now I'm at your old apartment."

"How? Never mind. It's getting dark. Stay right there. I'll come get you. The Control team will be out soon to search for any survivors."

"Okay. I'll stay. I love you."

Silence.

"I love you too," he said. Then there was a click.

"He's coming to get me," she mumbled. "The love of my life... I'll see him again."

Her mind raced as she considered the complicated situation she was in. Like a twisted dream. She needed to maintain the façade, be the Amelia from this world. The one who was presumably married to this version of Silas. She couldn't risk revealing her true self, not when her own world had seemingly fallen into chaos. She looked around his apartment once more, trying to gather herself.

After about an hour, she got a call. "Hello?"

"Come down and hurry," Silas said. "The sun is setting."

She ran down the steps as fast as she could, busted through the stair door, and stumbled out the front of the building. There it was. A beat-up pickup truck. She ran to it, and there he was in the driver's seat. Silas.

She got in and kissed him. He kissed her back.

"Where have you been, Amelia?" he asked. "We were getting worried."

"We?" she asked.

He looked at her, confused. "Yes. Me and Jack. ...our son?"

"A son? I have a son in this world?" she said aloud, although she meant for it to be a thought.

His eyebrows scrunched together as he started to drive. "Did you hit your head or something?"

She laughed. "No. But I need you to hear me out, okay? Listen to what I have to say because it's going to sound like I've lost my mind, but I promise I haven't."

She went into a brief background of everything that had happened: creating the time machine, the president visiting, Silas going into the past and future, the president's attack on the facility, the second attack on the cult, and his death.

He slammed on the brakes. "You want me to believe all of this? This sounds wild."

She looked at him with sincere eyes and all seriousness. "It's the truth, Silas. I promise. I'm not your Amelia. Well, this body is, but the subconscious is not. I believe it works like the time machine had, but instead of through time, this machine sends us to a different reality or universe or something. I think that's what the numbers at the end of each coordinate mean."

He started driving again. The sun was getting lower; they still had a ways to go.

"Okay. If I were to believe this, why are you here?" he asked.

She sighed. "Because we were testing the modified machine with the schematics you, well, *my* Silas brought back. The world back in my reality isn't like this though." She hesitated, looking out the window. "None of this happened."

"So how long are you here for?" he asked.

She thought about it. "I don't know. I don't know how to get back."

The truck lurched forward as a vehicle that had its headlights off hit it from behind. The truck swerved some, but Silas straightened it out and floored it. The other vehicle's headlights turned on and shined right into their eyes.

"Come on. Come on," he told the truck, wishing it would go faster.

But it didn't.

Shots thudded into the truck. He swerved on and off the road, down different streets, and up onto the highway. But the vehicle behind them didn't give up. It sped up, driving up next to them. More bullets hit the truck. Adrenaline and fear caused both Silas and Amelia to sweat. She didn't keep her eyes off him either.

She wasn't going to lose him again.

As he drove, his eyes moved in all directions, and his fast arms followed. Bullets pelted the truck once more. All she could think of was how much she loved this man, the man that—

Her vision went black as one of the rounds hit her rib cage, which in turn hit her heart.

6

The Sixth Chapter: Home

Darkness wrapped around Amelia like linen, suffocating her. It muffled sound as well. Yet after a few moments, there was sound: The dripping sound of The Echo Machine. The humming of its medical equipment. The crunch of Jesse eating chips. The soft intake of her breathing.

She opened her eyes, and the room's light felt like daggers to her eyes. "We really need to move the light, so it's not directly hitting people when they wake up..."

"Amelia!" Jesse ran over to the table. "You're back!"

The smell of BBQ chips hit her nose. "Yeah... I'm back." She attempted to sit up, but her head spun. "How long was I out?"

He gently assisted her into a sitting position. "For about an hour or two. How long did it feel to you?"

"It felt like I was there for roughly six to eight hours," she responded.

"Drink this." He handed her a glass of water and waited until she set the glass down to speak again. "Where were you?"

"Here. But it wasn't here. The building was destroyed, and Jason King had taken over. Silas...Silas was alive, and I had red hair, but it was still me. We...we were married."

Jesse hung onto every word she said.

"I think I was in a different reality or universe or something because it wasn't our Earth. I think the numbers at the end of a coordinate has to do with it." She shook her head as the room spun. "The *N* and *W*... Like that was Earth 3125."

He unhooked the IV and the wires and grabbed another drink to wet her pallet.

She took a sip. "I wonder if we could change those numbers. Maybe it would take us to a different reality."

He was still lost in everything she said. Travel time didn't faze him. Not at all. But different *realities?*

"So, what you're telling me is that there are other realities out there?" he said. "Like, say, there is a version where we might all be frog people?"

She nodded as she took another sip of her drink. "I don't know about frog people, but maybe... I think we should look into this more." She tried getting out of bed, but she fumbled, so he helped her. Once she was on her feet, she waved him off, stretched, and paced around the room. "Do you realize what we have done? If this is all true, we have accomplished something that no one has ever been able to achieve...again."

He nodded and blankly stared at the ground, absorbing everything.

She sat and buried her face in her hands. "I know it's shocking. Trust me. I was there, and I still don't believe it."

He leaned over the table, wrote words on a piece of paper, picked it up, and used a piece of tape to stick it to the wall.

She looked over at the piece of paper. "E3125?"

"You've been through a lot. We're putting a pin in it for today. We'll work on this tomorrow." With a smile, he helped her up by her arm.

"I'm okay, Jesse. I mean it. I can walk, and I feel much better."

But he wouldn't let her argue with him. "No. We aren't going to push ourselves too hard on this. Go home. I'm going home. Let's just relax for the rest of the day, okay?"

She hesitated but nodded.

"How about this? Come over for dinner and bring Lucy. It'll be a lot of fun."

She liked that idea. "Okay. Let me run home first and grab her."

She stopped by the store to pick up a premade salad, ran home, found a large mixing bowl, dumped it in there, covered it with plastic wrap, grabbed Lucy, and left to head to Jesse's. As she drove with Lucy in the back seat, she couldn't help but let her thoughts drift, reflecting on the whirlwind of events. The prospect of parallel realities being real. The implications weighed on her mind.

"How could we use this?" she muttered. "What applications could we derive from this?"

When she arrived at Jesse's house, Lucy was pacing in the back seat, eager to greet him and his family. She opened the car door, and the dog jumped out and ran to Jesse's door. Jesse opened it and welcomed her in. Inside, the aroma of a savory meal filled the air. The warm ambiance provided comfort after the tumultuous day.

Over dinner, the conversation returned to their extraordinary findings. They discussed The Echo Machine's potential uses, the significance of the mysterious 3125, and the possibilities of exploring different realities. Amelia and Jesse's excitement fueled the discussion. As the evening progressed, the debate expanded from ethics to exploration and various types of worlds that might exist.

"Don't take this the wrong way or anything," Sandra, Jesse's wife, said. "I mean this with care, but what gives you both the right to use this? Again, I don't mean that in a negative way. I'm genuinely curious. You already have machines that can travel through time, and now you have a machine that can traverse parallel universes?"

Jesse and Amelia sat there, looking at each other.

"I don't know. I don't even know how we can use this," Amelia said. "What if our actions in one reality inadvertently affect others? How do we ensure we don't disrupt the delicate balance of different worlds?"

Jesse nodded thoughtfully. "You both are right. We need to approach this with caution and responsibility. It's not just about what we can do but what we *should* do."

As the night went on, they ended up talking about day-to-day life and various other topics to keep their minds occupied. Lucy played with Jesse's daughter in the backyard. As it grew late, Amelia decided it was time for her to leave and said her goodbyes. And so did her pup. She let Jesse know she would see him at work in the morning.

The drive back home was peaceful with the quiet night surrounding her and Lucy. As she entered her home, she couldn't help but feel a sense of gratitude for Jesse, who had become an integral part of her life. She was fortunate to have such a supportive friend by her side.

Amelia settled into her evening routine, taking care of Lucy and reflecting on the day's events. The Echo Machine had opened a door to uncharted territories, and she was ready to step through it.

The next day, Amelia hopped up to start her day. On the way

to work, she stopped at the local donut shop and picked up two coffees and several boxes of donuts for the break room. When she dropped off the boxes in the break room, she grabbed some for herself and Jesse. He was already in the machine's room.

"Thank you," he said as he saw the coffee and donuts in her hands.

She sat next to him, and they drank their coffee, ate their donuts, and pondered their next move—whether to explore further or to figure out how this discovery could be put to use. The morning sunlight streamed through the window, casting a warm glow on their faces. A brief serene moment.

"Jesse, I've been giving a lot of thought to The Echo Machine and its implications," she said, breaking the silence. Determination filled her eyes. "We have a profound responsibility here. I believe we should explore it, considering the possibilities it might unveil. We could make groundbreaking discoveries in various fields. Like medical technology."

He nodded, his expression deep in thought. "You're right. I also think it's crucial to assemble a team of experts from various disciplines—physicists, ethicists, medical scientists, and more. However, before we do that, we should determine if the machine can indeed transport us to other worlds. I think we need to make another attempt but with a different set of coordinates."

She nodded.

They continued brainstorming about potential team members and searched through their paperwork to see if there were any hints or clues for other coordinates. After a few hours of searching, they couldn't find any additional numbers.

"I guess we could consider randomizing the numbers," she said. "Perhaps selecting our favorite numbers and seeing where they lead us."

He nodded, liking this idea. "Should we stick with four digits?"

She pondered this. "Yeah. Maybe we should. How about we use both of our birthdays? Mine is on the fourteenth, and yours is on the twenty-eighth."

He chuckled. "Why not?"

He started up the machine, and she modified the code to change the coordinates to end in 1428. This process only took a few minutes.

"Do you want to go this time?" she asked.

He turned around. "Sure. I want to see what other worlds there are."

She strapped him into the machine and plugged him in. The machine tapped, lights blinked, and the machine's rumblings grew louder.

"Good luck," she said.

Then all was silent.

7

The Seventh Chapter: Escape

The sounds of breathing with the assistance of a medical pump, the beeping from a heart rate monitor, the dripping of antibiotics and saline bags, and the tapping of a shoe—these weren't normal sounds one would hear on an average day. But then again, this wasn't a typical day.

Silas looked around but couldn't call out for help. He gazed down his body, and at the end of the bed stood the man responsible for putting him here, Jason King.

"Thought you would never wake up," Jason said. "Didn't think you would even make it to the hospital. But oh, I'm so glad you did. We have so much to do." He grinned, his words laced with a sinister tone. "I hope there are no hard feelings between us though. I mean, business is business, and you were getting in the way. I'm sure you would have done the same if I got in your way."

He struggled to get up. His injuries' pain pulsed through his body, a constant reminder.

"No, no, no. Don't do that. Can't have you ripping your stitches or injuring yourself more. Now, here's the thing, you shouldn't be afraid of me. I don't know why you were in the first place—after *protecting* you and everything. But still, I'm not the president anymore. I left because of the predicament you, your friends, and my daughter put me in. It made it hard to cover all this up. But don't worry. You still have me—your new best friend."

The room remained an unsettling mix of mechanical and medical sounds, a constant reminder that this was no ordinary day for Silas. He struggled against the grogginess that clung to him, trying to make sense of his surroundings. The words of Jason King echoed in his ears.

He desperately looked around. Wanting to call for help. To escape this nightmare. But his body refused. Helpless, vulnerable, and trapped. The heart rate monitor continued its monotonous beeping, a stark contrast to the turmoil in his mind.

His gaze shifted downward. Jason King still stood at the end of the bed. Jason's calm demeanor only added to the sense of dread that washed over him. He wanted to protest his new, enigmatic "friend"—to defend himself—but his body remained unresponsive.

"Oh, you must be wondering what happened to your little girlfriend and Jesse," Jason continued. "They're fine, I guess. I really don't know. For all I know, they're probably in a ditch somewhere. Shame. She was a pretty little thing, wasn't she? I kind of wish I had her in this bed instead of you, but I guess it is what it is. Anyway, you heal up there. We will come pick you up soon. I've got a list of items that need to be taken care of before you come home."

Silas clenched his fists beneath the sheets, his mind racing with a mixture of anger, fear, and determination. He understood that, for the time being, he had to comply with Jason's plans. Bide his time and gather any information that might help him and his friends.

Silas opened his mouth to speak, but the presence of a tube down his throat rendered him unable to do so.

Jason noticed this. "No, don't say anything." A smirk crossed his face. "Well, you can't. You have a tube down your throat." He turned to the door. Before leaving the room, he turned and glanced at Silas from the door frame. "Oh, it's been a few months. They think you're dead. I sent them a letter, but they didn't believe you were alive. So, they had a funeral."

The door closed behind him, and his footsteps echoed in the sterile hospital environment.

As Silas lay there, the weight of his situation pressed down on him, his mind racing. A hollow ache filled his heart at the thought of the pain Amelia and Jesse must have gone through. He *had* to find a way to let them know he was still alive. That he hadn't given up.

He assessed his surroundings more thoroughly, noting the medical equipment and the room's layout. It was clear he was in a hospital, but which one and where?

His thoughts raced. He needed to gather information about Jason's operation, assess the hospital's security, and identify any potential allies. Yet the more he planned, the more drained his body became. His eyes became heavy like sandbags. Exhaustion overcame him, even though he hadn't moved.

As Silas slipped into a fitful sleep, his mind continued to churn. In his dreams, he found himself lying next to Amelia. In a hotel room. As he looked around, he spotted a wedding dress on the floor, along with a tuxedo. In the next scene, they both stood in front of their new house on a vast stretch of land, and soon, they had children.

But Amelia got in a car wreck. She was in the hospital. He visited her daily, but one fateful day, he found Jason King in the hospital room with an empty syringe. In a panic, Jason fled, and he chased after him. No matter how hard he tried, he was always just a step behind, unable to catch Jason.

Silas woke up in a sweat, silently screaming with the tube still in his throat. He lay there, drenched, until morning came.

The echoes of his dream still lingered in his mind as morning light filtered into the room. A shiver crawled down his spine. But as the reality of his situation set in once more. He had no time to dwell on dreams or fears.

The familiar sounds of medical equipment lingered, and in the background, the shuffles of the hospital staff going about their duties drifted in and out. As he lay there, footsteps approached from outside the door, growing louder.

Jason.

Panic welled within him, yet he had to maintain his composure. The footsteps continued growing louder until they halted. A shadow rested outside the door, and after a moment, a knock sounded.

His doctor.

"Good morning, Mr. Jarred Smith," the doctor said as he stepped inside. "I'm here to check your chart and see how you're feeling today. I'm glad you're awake. You had a nasty accident."

Silas lay there, puzzled. Jarred Smith? Why was he calling him that?

"Let's take a look." He retrieved Silas's charts and examined the monitoring machines. "So far, everything is looking good. Let me check those gunshot wounds." He lifted Silas's gown and lowered the blanket to inspect the wounds. "They are healing quite well. You were very close to death. Thank goodness the former president noticed you were injured and brought you in. Isn't he a wonderful man? He mentioned you worked at his favorite coffee shop. Unfortunately, we couldn't find your ID."

He remained perplexed. Yet he theorized Jason must've given the doctor a false name to cover his tracks in case Jesse or Amelia were looking for him.

The doctor placed the clipboard on Silas's lap. "All right, Mr. Smith. This is going to be very uncomfortable, but I'm going to remove the tube from your mouth. It's going to hurt to talk for an hour or two, but I'll have a nurse bring in some water and numbing spray to help with that."

He nodded.

The doctor donned gloves, unclipped the device holding the tube in place, and pulled. He hadn't lied; it was indeed uncomfortable. Silas's body tensed from the pain, and he coughed and gagged. Finally, it was done.

"Alrighty," the doctor said. "I'll let the former president know you should be good and cleared to leave this evening. I'll come check on you one more time later this afternoon to give you a final say. The nurse will be in soon with the water and numbing spray."

Silas nodded again and attempted to say *thank you* but was unable to do so because of the discomfort—like tiny cuts everywhere—in his throat.

The doctor left, leaving the door open.

A few minutes later, a nurse walked in with some water and spray. She helped him sip his water and sprayed the numbing spray in his mouth. She also brought some ice chips to help. He thanked her the best he could with his numb throat. When she left, she let him know she would bring food in a bit, which had to be in liquid form but only for the day.

She returned with chicken broth, a smoothie, and apple juice about thirty minutes later. The broth felt amazing and tasted wonderful, as did the smoothie. Although the apple juice was a bit too sweet for his liking, he still drank it.

Now full with his energy returning, he looked around his room. There weren't any windows. He spotted a bag of his clothes, but the clothes were cut up and bloody. All he had on was a gown.

Figuring no one else would be coming in for a while, he decided to give standing a try. He slowly swung his legs over the edge of the bed, pain shooting up from where he had been shot in his left thigh and chest. But he ignored it.

He counted to three and gradually put his feet on the ground. Dizziness swarmed him. He pushed through, holding onto a rail to maintain his balance. It took a few minutes, but he was standing—although his legs felt weak.

He considered attempting to walk and decided to try. He placed his right leg forward and then brought his injured leg to meet his right one. Pain from torn muscles shot through the wounded leg. He clenched his jaw, grinding his teeth. But he couldn't stop. He repeated this motion, right leg forward followed by the left leg meeting the right. For about thirty minutes, he kept going, gradually getting the hang of it while using his IV bag holder as support, even though he was drenched in sweat from the pain.

He made his way to the door and peeked outside. It seemed relatively quiet for the morning, but he had no idea what day it was. He decided to venture out and down the hallway, creeping along one foot at a time with his IV bag holder. He passed several rooms with patients inside and had to frequently pause because of the overwhelming pain. Eventually, he found a patient who was asleep and quietly entered the room, except for his heavy panting. He sat in a chair, took several deep breaths, and scanned the patient's room.

He noticed a small dresser nearby. The patient remained sound asleep. He realized this might be his only chance.

He removed the IV from his arm, discarded the gown, and saw his wounds for the first time. They were stitched and stapled up with small bandages covering them. He put on pants and a hoodie he found, ripping off the medical bracelet as well. He glanced around the room, found a pair of Chucks, and slipped them on. After placing the IV bag holder in the bathroom, he threw the gown and medical bracelet into a trash can.

He limped to the door and looked around, making sure the coast was clear. He then took a left and proceeded down the hallway. He found a window that looked outside, realizing he was a few floors up and in an unfamiliar area.

An exit sign led to a staircase. After pushing through the doors, he slowly made his way down the steps, each step increasing the pain in his leg. He eventually reached the first floor and peered through the door, which led to a parking garage. Perfect.

He limped through the garage. As he approached the exit, vehicles approached, and he ducked behind a nearby car. Three solid black SUVs pulled into the garage, each adorned with little American flags. Jason. He needed to hurry.

The vehicles continued up the parking garage, and he limped out of hiding and glanced around, trying to orient himself on where to go. Then it hit him.

He could call Terry.

As he walked down the street, he spotted a stranger nearby. "Excuse me. I'm so sorry to bother you, but I'm quite lost. Do you know what city we are in?"

The stranger looked puzzled. "Huh? Oh, we are in DC, sir. Are you okay?"

He nodded. "Yes, I'm fine. Do you know how to get to the National Arboretum from here?"

The stranger pulled out his phone, checked the maps, and then showed him the route. "Here." He pointed at his phone. "Go down this road for about four blocks, take a right, go down three blocks, and then take a left. You'll go down that one for about five blocks, and you should be in the area."

Silas studied the map. "Thank you."

As he turned to walk away, the stranger asked, "Do you want me to call you a cab or something?"

Silas turned around and shook his head. "I'm sorry, sir. I don't have my wallet on me."

The stranger looked Silas over. "Here. I'll call a cab and give you some cash for it. That's too far to walk, especially while injured." He pointed at Silas's leg. "I don't want you to argue. Just take it."

Silas looked around, suspicious of the stranger's kindness, but eventually accepted and thanked the man.

As they waited for the cab, they engaged in conversation. The stranger pulled out a cigarette and offered one to Silas, who declined. They chatted about their families and what they did. Silas grew nervous, knowing Jason was likely in the building. Hopefully, the former president was still getting to his room.

When the cab arrived, Silas provided the address, and the stranger handed the cab driver the cash. Silas thanked him multiple times, but the stranger waved him off.

"I've needed help in the past, and someone was always there," the stranger said. "I just want to pass on the good that was given to me. Now go."

The cab drove away.

Silas glanced out the rear window and noticed hospital guards running out of the parking lot and looking around. He ducked, hoping they hadn't seen him. The cab smelled of cigarettes and a distinct lack of deodorant, but he couldn't have been happier because this smell meant he was finally free.

Yet he still had an underlying feeling that Jason would come after him soon.

As the cab continued, it approached a familiar street.

"Which house, sir?" the cab driver asked.

Silas looked out the window. "Keep going." He soon spotted the house he was looking for but asked the driver to stop at the one four houses down. He got out of the cab, thanked the driver, and watched as the cab drove away. Looking around, he didn't see anything unusual. Limping, he made his way down the sidewalk and to Terry's house.

As he walked, he wondered if Terry knew if I was alive or not. At Terry's front door, he knocked and waited. A few minutes later, no response.

He knocked again, but still, there was no sign of anyone. He peered through the window. The lights were off. He figured Terry might be out grocery shopping or so, so he decided to wait by the door, trying to stay out of view from the street.

Yet his heart raced. The minutes dragged on, and he couldn't shake the feeling of vulnerability. Jason and his guards were out there, looking for him, and with every passing moment, his risk of being found increased. Pain from his wounds also intensified as the drugs had finally worn off.

To keep his mind off it all, he reminisced about his time with Amelia, the moments they had shared and the night he had proposed. They had kept it a secret, wanting to savor the joy for themselves without complicating the mission at hand.

With every passing car, his heart rate still spiked, and he tensed. The sun beat down on him, causing sweat to bead on his forehead. Despite the pain, the heat, and the vulnerable situation, he couldn't help but notice the beauty of the outdoors—the birds singing, the squirrels chirping. A stark contrast to the turmoil inside him.

A car approached the house and sat idle. Fear gripped him. The engine then shut off. Nothing else moved. His mind wondered how Jason had already found him. He scanned his surroundings, realizing that his best chance of escape might involve a fight. However, his injuries limited his abilities.

Footsteps approached, coming up the steps. Then a gasp.

"Silas? Is that really you?" Terry asked, his voice breaking through the tension.

Silas's racing heart slowed as he recognized his friend standing there with grocery bags. "Yeah, it's me." Exhaustion and relief mixed inside his voice. "Please get me inside. I escaped from a hospital."

Terry unlocked the door, placed his groceries inside, and returned to help Silas to his feet. Silas winced. They entered the house, and he carefully seated Silas on the couch. He then went to the front door to check their surroundings before locking it. After putting away the groceries, he poured Silas a glass of ice water, brought it over, and settled into a chair opposite the couch, facing Silas.

"What happened, Silas?" Terry said, concern evident in his

voice. "Jesse told me his side when he carried Amelia out of there."

Silas looked over at him. "Were they hurt? Did anyone else get out?"

His expression saddened. "Not many people managed to escape. Almost all who showed up for the distraction were shot. I have no information about the facility's staff who helped you. Scarlet was shot but dropped off in front of the facility as a message to you all."

Silas's eyes looked away. "Is she okay?"

He offered a reassuring smile. "Yes. She's all right. She stayed here for a while to recover, but she's back home now. She's expanding the cult and searching for her father."

"Well, he's still around." Silas sighed. "I don't know where he's living, but he's here. I saw him last night, and he came to get me from the hospital. He mentioned that he still possesses copies of most of the stolen files. According to him, he wants to recreate the machine and asked for my help."

Silas then proceeded to recount everything, starting from getting shot until he arrived at Terry's house. They then sat in silence for a moment as Terry absorbed the entire story.

Terry noticed Silas grimacing. "Here. Let me get you some painkillers. They might not be as strong as the ones you had at the hospital, but they should help." He rose from his seat, went to a cabinet, and retrieved some painkillers from an old surgery supply. He also grabbed a couple of ice packs, which he placed on Silas's leg and chest. "These will help with the inflammation. I'll also call my doctor friend to get you bandages and to see if he'll check over your wounds tonight. Do you want to call Amelia and Jesse?"

Silas considered the question and then shook his head. "As

much as I want to, I don't know what Jason might do to them if I contacted them or returned. I need things to cool down, and I need to heal. I don't know how many people he still has under his control."

Terry nodded. "All right. You can stay here until you're feeling better. Let me get you something to eat." He got up and began preparing chicken noodle soup.

As he chopped vegetables and heated the broth, the comforting aroma wafted through the room, providing some solace to Silas.

"Have you heard from or about Amelia and Jesse?" Silas asked.

Terry glanced over. "I've heard how they've been from Scarlet, and they're doing all right. From what I hear, they've restarted their facility and started getting clients. Amelia mentioned that working helped heal the pain of losing you."

"Good. I was hoping she didn't fall into a depression and drink herself into a coma." Silas smiled, relieved his friends were doing okay and from Terry's help. Hopefully, Jason wouldn't find him until the time was right.

8

The Eighth Chapter: Heal

Silas groaned as he woke up, his muscles protesting with every movement. He winced, the pain from his wounds reminding him of the events that had unfolded just the day before. His chest and leg were still tender, and his bandages felt tight, but the worst of the bleeding had stopped. He slowly swung his legs off the bed, letting his feet touch the cool wooden floor before standing.

With a sigh, he shuffled to the bathroom, where he gingerly removed his bandages. His skin was pale, the fresh scars a painful reminder of the battle he'd survived. He ran a hand over his face, staring at himself in the mirror—eyes sunken, hair messy, his body bruised but alive.

As he walked downstairs, the smell of toasted bread hit him first, comforting in its familiarity. The kitchen was warm, and Terry was there, focused on the sizzling pan in front of him. Silas couldn't help but notice the small, careful movements Terry made, as if he was still worried about him.

Terry glanced over his shoulder, his brow furrowing as he spotted Silas. "Hey there. How's the leg? Need any help with the bandages?"

"I'm sore," Silas replied with a small smile, trying to mask the fatigue in his voice. "But I'll manage. Breakfast smells great." He gestured toward the plate of toast with honey and cottage cheese, a dish from his past he hadn't thought of in years.

Terry set the spatula down and placed a plate in front of Silas. "You're welcome. I know it's not much, but I figured it might bring back some memories."

Silas sat at the table, taking a bite of the toast. The sweetness of the honey and the tang of the cottage cheese were a strange comfort. "It's perfect. Just like the old days." He paused, swallowing. "Thank you. You've done a lot for me. I wish there was something I could do to repay you."

Terry shook his head, his smile warm. "You don't owe me anything, Silas. I just want to help. But... what's your plan from here?"

Silas leaned back, his fingers tracing the rim of his coffee cup. "Honestly? I don't know. I guess I'll leave when you're ready to kick me out." He gave a dry laugh, though it didn't reach his eyes.

Terry's expression softened. "When you're ready to go, I can drive you to Scarlet's place. From there, she can help you get home. But take your time, okay? Focus on healing. The rest can wait."

"Thanks. Hopefully, by then, Jason will have given up on me," Silas muttered, his thoughts darkening.

"You're not alone in this, Silas. We'll make sure you're safe." Terry's voice was steady, a reassurance Silas desperately needed.

Silas took a deep breath, meeting Terry's gaze. "Thank you.

You've been a lifesaver. I don't know what I would've done without you."

The days passed slowly, but Terry's care was steady. Silas healed a little more each day, though the weight of the situation still hung over him. His body was mending, but his mind was still heavy. He spent his days in silence, feeling trapped by the weight of what was coming.

It was late one evening when the phone rang, its shrill sound breaking the silence. Terry's voice was grim when he spoke. "That was Scarlet. They've got a lead on Jason. It's time."

Silas's heart raced. This was it. This could be the turning point, the chance to stop Jason once and for all. But as he heard Terry's words, a dark premonition crept into his gut.

"I'm driving you to Scarlet's," Terry said, gathering his keys. "You need to be there when things go down."

The plan was simple. It was supposed to be simple.

Silas was halfway down the road when everything changed.

A sharp crack shattered the quiet night. His head whipped around, his heart dropping to his stomach. He slammed on the brakes, his hands gripping the wheel as the sound of gunfire echoed in the distance.

Terry was hit.

The shock left Silas frozen for a split second. His mind screamed for action, but his body felt leaden. He jerked the car off the road and slammed it into park, his breath coming in ragged gasps.

He scrambled out of the car, rushing toward Terry's house, panic surging through him.

When he reached the door, his hands shook as he fumbled for the handle. He burst inside, heart in his throat. His eyes scanned the living room, but there was no sign of Terry. The silence was suffocating.

"Terry?" he called hoarsely.

A soft groan echoed from the hallway.

Silas ran toward the sound, his breath catching in his chest. He found Terry in the kitchen, blood staining the floor beneath him. His body was limp, but his eyes—those eyes—still held some flicker of life.

"Silas," Terry rasped, his voice barely above a whisper. "Get out of here. You... can't stay. They'll be here... any minute."

"No," Silas protested, kneeling beside him. "I won't leave you."

Terry's hand weakly reached for his. "You don't have a choice. You need to go. For Amelia. For Jesse. Don't let them find you."

Tears welled in Silas's eyes as he felt the life drain from his friend's hand. "I'm sorry. I'm so sorry."

With one final breath, Terry went still.

Silas's world collapsed. He couldn't stay here. He couldn't risk Jason finding him at the house. But he couldn't leave Terry like this, either.

He called 911 from an anonymous line, reporting the gunshots and the emergency. It was all he could do.

Silas drove into the night, his hands trembling on the steering wheel. His mind spun in a haze, grief clawing at his chest. The memories of Terry, the man who had taken him in, fed him, cared for him... all gone in an instant.

But there was no time to mourn. He had to keep moving.

His phone buzzed. Scarlet's name lit up the screen. He answered, voice tight.

"Silas? What's going on? Are you okay?" Her voice crackled with concern.

"I... Terry's gone," he whispered, unable to hold back the

weight of the words. "I had to leave. Jason... He's still after me."

"Damn it," Scarlet cursed. "Get to me. Now. I'll help you, just get here."

Silas nodded, though she couldn't see him. "I'm on my way."

Hours passed, and Silas found himself pushing through the night, the miles slipping away behind him. He barely noticed the passage of time. All he could think of was the road ahead, and the woman waiting for him at the end.

When he finally pulled into Hot Springs, his relief was palpable. He drove through the gate, his body tense as he navigated the winding path that led to Scarlet's place. There she was, waiting for him outside, her arms open.

Silas didn't hesitate. He got out of the car, walking toward her with an overwhelming sense of gratitude.

"I'm glad you made it," Scarlet said, her voice gentle. "You're safe now."

She pulled him into a hug, and for the first time in what felt like forever, Silas allowed himself to relax.

Later that night, after a quiet meal and some much-needed rest, they sat together, discussing everything. Scarlet had news about Jason, but it wasn't good. His operation was bigger than they had imagined.

"You don't need to be part of this, Silas," she said. "You need to go home. Let me handle this. You've got other people to protect."

Silas shook his head. "I can't sit back. I won't."

They argued for a while, but in the end, Scarlet gave him a choice.

"You can leave in the morning, go back to Amelia and Jesse. Or you can stay here. But either way, you need to decide."

The next morning, Silas made his choice. He'd go home. It wasn't time to fight Jason yet. He had to take care of what mattered most.

When he left in the morning, Scarlet handed him a full tank of gas and a bag of supplies for the road.

"Stay safe," she said, a teasing glint in her eye. "And go see your girl, lover boy."

Silas smiled, his heart pounding at the thought of Amelia. He got in the car, grateful for the chance to see her again.

As he drove, the city's familiar sights came into view. He could almost taste the reunion. His heart raced as he parked, glancing into the rearview mirror to steady himself. He wanted to look like nothing had changed, like nothing had happened.

But he knew it had.

With a deep breath, he opened the door, and walked inside to the woman he loved.

9

The Ninth Chapter: Reunion

The Echo Machine, with its array of computers and intricate machinery, stood ready for another journey into the unknown.

As Amelia and Jesse input the coordinates to world 1999 and activated the machine, the room filled with a low hum, and their anticipation grew. The possibilities were endless as the machine tapped into the fabric of parallel realities.

A voice spoke behind them.

Assuming it was just another employee, Jesse said, "Please wait. We're in the middle of something." Yet when he turned his head around and saw who it was, he couldn't believe his eyes. Urgency filled his voice. "Amelia, turn around."

Puzzled, she didn't move, still mostly focused on her work. He spun her chair around, and her mouth dropped open.

"You're...you're seeing this too, Jesse?" she asked, her eyes welling with tears.

He nodded.

She slowly stood, tears streaming down her cheeks. She ran up to the person who had just entered the room—and slapped him.

"What the hell, Silas?!" she cried, her emotions overwhelming her. "Where have you been?! Why haven't you called?! The hell, Silas! We *buried* you!"

He didn't resist as she slapped him once more, understanding that it was only an outpouring of love, not hate. He then wrapped his arms around her as she cried. Her tears soaked his chest.

"I'll tell you both in a little bit," he said softly. "I missed you, Amelia. I love you."

She kept crying, unable to catch her breath. Slowly, she fell to her knees, and he gently lowered himself with her, holding her tightly.

"Why?" she whispered through her tears. She kissed his neck and face. "Why did you have to do that?"

He held her close, his own eyes glistening with tears. He wiped her tears away with his thumb. "I'm so sorry. It's a long story, and I promise I'll explain everything. But right now, I just want to be with you."

Jesse, who had been silently watching the emotional reunion, stepped forward. "We've got a lot of catching up to do." A warm smile stretched across his face. "But first, let's give her a moment."

She clung to Silas, her grip slowly relaxing as her sobs subsided. Her eyes looked up at him with a mixture of disbelief and relief. "I–I thought you were gone forever," she whispered, her voice trembling.

Silas held her face in his hands and kissed her forehead. "I promise I'll never leave you like that again."

As they embraced, the weight of the past months lifted, replaced by the warmth of their love and the hope of a future together. It was a moment they had all thought was impossible, but there they were—reunited again against all odds.

Eventually, they all settled down, taking a seat. Silas recounted his incredible journey, from his hospital escape to Terry and his reunion with Scarlet. Amelia and Jesse listened with rapt attention, interjecting with questions and expressions of astonishment.

After he updated them on everything, they talked about everything they had done: the clients they had gotten, the Future Project file they had delved into, and the worlds they had visited, all with the help of *his* file.

He couldn't help but feel proud of them for thriving in his absence. A bittersweet moment. "Did you manage to alter the machine to the new coding? Where did you go?"

"We found different universes where things had changed slightly," Amelia responded. "One where Jesse wasn't married, another where Jason King was emperor and had destroyed most of the Earth, and another where I only had nine fingers due to an accident. Weird things like that. We were about to go on another adventure today, but we need to set up a schedule where we start at Earth 0001 and then move up. To coordinate it with our work."

"Wow... That's amazing. Have you started writing descriptions of the places you've gone to yet?"

"Yeah," Jesse replied. "Not super detailed but enough."

Silas considered this. "But still, it's exciting. I'd like to sit in on one if that's okay."

He and Amelia exchanged looks.

"Of course, Silas," she said. "This is your project as well. We'll start one here in a little bit."

Silas smiled and hugged them both again.

As they began their work, he observed closely, following along with their process. She climbed into the machine, and Jesse hooked her up, turned on the machine, and connected the code.

"Ready?" Jesse asked.

She nodded with a smile and winked at Silas.

He clicked Enter to run the program. The machine hummed loudly, lights blinked and flashed, and the noise grew louder and louder until it all stopped. And Amelia was gone.

"You should have a seat," he said. "Sometimes, it takes a while."

Silas walked over to the chair next to him and sat.

"I'm glad you're back, Silas. I really am. And I'm sorry for everything that has happened to you. I want you to know we didn't know what to do." He handed Silas a letter, the same one they had gotten from the former president. The same one he always held onto since that day. "We didn't know what was real. She was in distress for a long time. It took her a while to heal. But I know she's so happy for you to be back."

Silas opened the letter and looked at the photo of himself, still a bit shocked. He read the letter, letting the words sink in. After a moment of reflection, he folded the letter and carefully placed it back into the envelope.

"Thank you, Jesse. I know it was a tough situation for the both of you, and I don't blame you for anything." His voice was filled with understanding. "I'm just glad to be back here with the both of you."

Jesse patted Silas's shoulder. "It's good having you back, bud."

Silas smiled but then asked, "Do you think Jason will show up here?"

He thought about it for a moment. "I don't think so. He hasn't yet."

Silas nodded. "Scarlet *did* say she has people watching over us."

They sat there for a few hours. Jesse eventually offered to get them drinks and food. Silas agreed and watched as he left the room.

As he sat there, Silas couldn't help but reflect on Amelia—his love, his partner, his everything. Her presence filled him with warmth. He had missed her deeply. He wheeled his chair over to her side, gently taking her hand in his. Her warm touch sent shivers down his spine. He leaned in and pressed his lips to her hand, savoring the moment.

Jesse walked in on Silas holding her hand. He didn't make a sound. Just stood there, giving them a moment. After a few minutes, he walked in and said, "Here you go, Silas." He handed him his drink and food.

They continued to sit there for a few more hours, waiting around.

Jesse then checked the clock, noticing it was almost five. "Hey, Silas. It's about that time when she would go let her dog out, but since she's under, I'll go ahead and do that. Just keep an eye on her. I'll be back in about an hour. Call me if you have any issues."

Silas nodded. "Sounds good. Oh, hey. Is her phone in here? I don't have mine. I only have a burner because of...everything."

He nodded, grabbed her phone from a desk, and handed it to Silas before saying goodbye.

Silas watched him leave, and as the minutes ticked by, he couldn't help but feel a mix of emotions. The room was quiet, except for the machine's soft hum and the keyboard's occasional click as he checked on their progress. Her breathing remained steady and peaceful.

With her phone, he decided to take a moment to text Scarlet, updating her on his return and current situation. He thanked her for her support again and vowed to stay in touch. Afterward, he set the phone aside and resumed his watchful eye over her.

He gently brushed her hair behind her ear and rested his head on her chest, listening to the rhythm of her heartbeat. Each beat filled him with a deep sense of contentment. The scent of her perfume, a delicate lavender with a hint of citrus, wafted around them. He hadn't initially been a fan of lavender, but over time, it had grown on him.

With a gentle stroke of his thumb, he brushed her cheek, feeling her smooth skin beneath his touch. Unbeknownst to him, he drifted off into slumber, where his dreams painted a picture of a future with her. They had grown old together and shared a morning on their porch, sipping coffee and watching the sunrise while a cool breeze kissed their faces.

A gentle touch to his face startled him awake. Blinking away the sleep, he realized it was Amelia, her hand still resting on his cheek. "How long?" he asked, trying to gauge the passage of time.

"I just woke up a minute or two ago," she replied.

"A couple of hours," Jesse chimed in from behind him.

Silas sat up, eager to help her disconnect from the machine. As she recounted her experiences on the other Earth, describing its futuristic wonders, he couldn't help but be amazed. This alternate reality featured hovering cars and an advanced reliance on magnetic power. He marveled at a world where peace had prevailed thanks to an abundance of free, non-sellable energy.

"Sadly, I don't think that will fly too well here," he said.

They all shared a hearty laugh and proceeded to document their findings.

When the paperwork was complete, Jesse suggested, "Let's call it a day. You can go home, and I'll finish up here."

Silas looked over at Amelia with a large smile. The trials of Jason could wait. For that night, they had each other.

10

The Tenth Chapter: Restoration

"What are we going to do now?" Captain Joel asked.

Across the table from him, Jason King sat, tapping his finger on the outside of his glass. "What do you mean?" His tone was sharp. "You let him get away. He was within your grasp, and you had to make a show of it by shooting the man harboring him. Of course, he ran away."

"You should have stationed some of my guards outside his room, like I had suggested, Jason," he snapped. "But you didn't listen, and he ran away from there as well."

Jason shot him a glance, his anger still evident. "Yes, you're right. But I didn't. I wanted him to trust me, and I thought his injuries would keep him from escaping. But I was wrong. It seems like I've been wrong about a lot of things lately."

"Well, at least we know where he will be heading to. Back to Jesse and Amelia. We can always snatch him from there."

Jason took a sip from his glass. "Snatch him? Why would we do that now? You're not thinking, you buffoon. If we snatch him, he will not work with us. He would rather take his own life than work with us. As of now, Silas Vale is off the table. We will need to outsource to get what I need done."

Joel sat there, nodding like a yes-man. "We'll find someone. Have you heard from Sarah and the girls?"

He finished his drink and threw the glass at Joel. It whizzed past his face and shattered on the wall behind him, sending shards in all directions.

"What do you think?!" Jason snapped, slamming his fist on the table. "Of course, I haven't! Ever since Scarlet, they took off! They want nothing to do with me! They think *I'm* the bad guy! But I am *far* from the bad guy!"

Joel simply sat there—undisturbed by the outburst. He then rose from his seat and made his way over to the liquor cabinet. With each step, glass crunched under his boot, a chilling reminder of the recent violence. He poured Jason another drink and placed it in front of the former president before settling back into his own seat.

"What do we do about those three?" he inquired, his voice laced with concern.

Jason's gaze shifted to his left, where the two guards who had accompanied Joel during their mission to retrieve Silas and the nurse who had been assigned to Silas sat, bound and seemingly emotionless. The nurse, her face stained with tears, had a rag in her mouth to muffle any sounds, but her distress was palpable.

He sighed, a mixture of irritation and frustration etching lines on his face. To him, they were mere inconveniences. Obstacles in his grand scheme.

He regarded Joel once more. "I'm sure the nurse won't say anything if we let her go, and your guards will learn from this mistake, right?"

Joel's response was a nonchalant shrug.

But he wasn't willing to take any chances.

In a swift, merciless motion, Jason seized the gun from the table and dispatched all three individuals. He then left the room, his parting words a harsh reminder of the consequences of their failures.

Joel was left to grapple with the gruesome aftermath, including the lifeless body of the nurse's husband in the living room.

Jason departed in his waiting vehicle, which was bound for his new residence registered under a fictitious company name. Frustration welled up within him. He knew he'd have to rewrite his plan and search for a new individual to build his machine, which meant additional time added to the overall goal. Despite this setback, he remained resolute. He made a few international calls, inquiring his contacts if they knew of anyone suitable for the task.

The phone calls continued after he got home, his mind already formulating a new strategy. He had a gift for connecting with people, knowing every detail about them. He took pride in establishing a personal rapport with these contacts, and more often than not, it played to his advantage. He would not let this minor setback deter him from achieving his goal.

Hours later, Jason sat in his living room when he received a call. "Hello?" he answered.

A cold voice on the other end responded. "Yes, it's me. I'm outside his house. What do you want me to do?"

He sat there, deep in thought on his next play against Captain Joel. "Is he home?"

"Yes, sir. He just parked his car and went inside."

"Just keep an eye on him. Don't do anything yet."

"Yes, sir."

The line went dead.

As he contemplated his moves, he couldn't help but feel a growing sense of paranoia and unease. Recent events and setbacks had shaken his once-unshakable confidence. He had to regain control of the situation and eliminate any potential threats.

He meticulously reviewed his options and considered new strategies. His mind operated like a chessboard, planning several moves ahead. The paranoia only serving to make him more resourceful.

Sitting in his dimly lit room, he stared at his laptop and the papers strewn across the table and floor. He then picked up his phone and called the man who had been watching Joel's house. "Is he still there?"

"Yes, sir," the man responded. "He's still there. Should I?"

Jason hesitated for only a moment. "Yes. Go ahead. It's time to remove any obstacles in our path."

"Yes, sir. The camera will be on."

He hung up and clicked a link that the man sent him. There, he could see outside of Joel's house. The man walked up to the house, proceeded to a trashcan near the house, climbed on top of it, and jumped onto the second-story balcony. He slid the balcony door open and stepped inside.

Upon entering, he looked over at the large bed, pulled out his pistol, and pointed it at the sleeping person. He fired off a few rounds. After completing the task, he called Jason. "Sir, it's taken care of."

"Show me the body," Jason said.

The man grabbed the comforter and pulled it down, revealing two men—those same two Control officers he had shot that day.

Anxiety grew within him. "Where's Joel?!"

Through the link, a loud gunshot rang, followed by a flash. The man fell to the floor. Another gunshot followed.

Joel walked up to the man, picked up the small camera, looked at it, bent down, and picked up the phone. "Hello, Jason," he said calmly. "You thought I wouldn't notice a man outside my house? Where do you think you've been getting your intel from since you've been out? Jason, you've grown weak and lost your way. And you better keep on your toes. Watch your back."

The call hung up, and Joel casually tossed the camera aside.

Jason seethed with anger. He grabbed his computer and hurled it across the room. The impact caused it to shatter. "Fuck!"

He sat there, heart racing and breathing heavy. His plan had failed, and now Joel would be coming after him. "Shit!"

He couldn't afford any more mistakes. His grand plan—his empire—was now at risk. He needed a new approach. A strategy to not only eliminate Joel but to ensure his own safety. He sat there, contemplating who he had left that he could reach out to.

He then picked up the phone and dialed a number he hadn't called in a while. The phone rang and rang. As he almost impatiently ended the call, a voice he hadn't heard in a long time spoke.

"Hello?" Sarah said.

His breath was taken away. "Sarah, it's me. Jason. Can I talk to the girls?"

Silence.

"I don't think that will be a good idea, Jason." She then hung up.

Jason collapsed onto the floor, having lost everything. He didn't even care if Joel walked through the door. He lay on the floor—until he fell asleep.

11

The Eleventh Chapter: E-0001

"Ready, Silas?" Jesse asked.

Strapped and hooked up to the machine, Silas looked over and nodded.

Amelia walked over and kissed him. "I'm ready, Jesse."

Jesse started the machine. Tapping and echoing. The tapping grew louder. The lights blinked and flashed, and a whooshing noise sounded as the tapping reached a thundering crescendo.

Then there was nothing.

Silas felt like he was falling and spinning, surrounded by a cacophony of noises. The sounds only grew louder but then stopped. Pressure pressed all around him. Then nothing.

"Silas, are you okay?" a voice said.

Silas opened his eyes and looked around. He lay in an empty building. "Where am I?" He looked over at the voice—Jesse.

"We've got to go, man," Jesse said. "They're coming."

He looked around. "What's coming?"

Jesse helped him to his feet. "You don't know? You must have hit your head pretty hard. Well, it's the undead."

His face dropped. "Un...dead?"

Jesse nodded. "Yeah, but they never died. There was that virus secretly released in a batch of aspirin, remember? It makes you angry and aggressive. Starts with a simple cough. Then you get migraines. Which leads people to take more aspirin. As time goes on, the side effects increase. Eventually, you become aggressive, your teeth and fingernails fall out, and you lose the feeling of pain. It wouldn't be so bad if there weren't millions of them. People died, and the economy collapsed. People had to fend for themselves. Now, we're here—hiding from these *people*.

"But the reason I said undead is because they're nearly impossible to kill since they feel no pain. They just keep coming. The rumor is that President King was the one who signed off on putting the virus in the medication."

Silas stood there in shock. "Where...where's Amelia?"

Jesse looked at him. "Who's Amelia?"

He didn't know what to say. She either didn't exist here, or they had no knowledge of her.

"We gotta go."

And off they went, sneaking out of the building. Jesse held a twelve-gauge shotgun, and Silas had a pistol.

"Where are we going?" Silas asked, astounded by the extent of changes in this world.

Jesse turned his head back as they walked down the street. "Man, you must have really bumped your head. You should get that checked out when we get back. We're heading to the family, the Cult of Sacred Bodies."

As they navigated through the desolate streets, the grim reality of this alternate world became increasingly apparent. The once-thriving city was now a shadow of its former self with dilapidated buildings, overgrown vegetation, and eerie silence.

Silas couldn't help but compare it to the world he knew, the one he had left behind.

Jesse continued to provide more information. The family were a fraction of survivors who had come together to protect themselves from the infected's relentless onslaught. Their mission was to safeguard humanity against those who had been twisted by the virus.

As they approached the city's outskirts, they reached a concealed entrance that led to an underground shelter. Jesse knocked on the door, using a specific pattern, and it slowly creaked open, revealing a group of wary but well-armed individuals. Recognizing Jesse, they granted entry to both of them.

Inside the underground sanctuary, Silas encountered a diverse group of survivors, each with their own harrowing tale of survival in this nightmarish world. But they were all united with a common purpose: to discover a cure for the virus and to rebuild society.

As he followed Jesse around the underground base, a woman he recognized approached them. "Hey, guys. How did it go?" Scarlet said.

Jesse proceeded to fill her in on their recent experiences, including Silas hitting his head.

She turned her attention to Silas. "Go see the medic and get that checked out."

Silas nodded, and she left.

As Jesse led him to the medic area, he couldn't help but be amazed at the number of people they had managed to accommodate underground. It was like an underground *city*. They approached the medic station, and one of the doctors stepped forward.

"Hey, doc," Jesse said. "My buddy Silas here bumped his

head pretty bad, and he doesn't remember much. Mind taking a look?"

The doctor led Silas to one of the examination tables and began a thorough checkup, inspecting his eyes, measuring his blood pressure, and feeling his head for any bumps. "From what I can tell, he doesn't have a large concussion, but he might have a minor one. Just keep an eye on him and"—he handed Silas a bag of pills—"take this. They're just ibuprofen." He grabbed a nearby drink. "Also, drink this. It won't taste great. Don't ask what's in it." He let out a chuckle.

Silas tried to down the drink , but the taste was awful. He instead forced himself to swallow the unpleasant concoction, grimacing as the taste lingered in his mouth. He washed it down with a gulp of water and nodded to the doctor. "Thanks," he managed to say, still wincing from the taste.

The doctor smiled warmly, understanding his discomfort. "No problem. Make sure you rest up. Head injuries can be tricky."

As they left the medic area, Jesse filled Silas in on more details about the underground community. It seemed that this place had become a refuge for people from all walks of life, each with their unique skills and contributions to the group. Some were scientists working on finding a cure, while others focused on security and maintaining the underground facilities.

Silas was impressed by their resilience and determination. He couldn't help but feel a sense of belonging among these survivors who were fighting to reclaim their world. But just as Jesse was about to take him to his living quarters, a boy ran up to them.

"Scarlet needs you!" the boy said. "She's in her meeting room." He then darted away.

"Great... What now?" Jesse said.

They jogged over to where Scarlet was. She stood over a map, examining it and communicating with someone over a walkie-talkie. She held up her pointer finger, indicating that she would be right with them.

"Okay. Great." She lowered the walkie-talkie and turned to Jesse and Silas. "Hey, you two. We have someone trapped in a building a few blocks away, and we need you two to go get her."

Jesse sighed. "Who is she?"

She pointed at a building on the map. "We don't know, but our scouts around the area have reported seeing someone in that building. An infected followed her to the location. So, get going."

Jesse looked at the map and walked away. Silas followed him to the armory, where they grabbed weapons and what appeared to be old SWAT gear for their arms and chests. They then headed out through the bunker doors, which shut behind them.

As they followed the given directions, they heard screaming and approaching footsteps. They quickly hid behind a burnt-out car. The footsteps grew closer, the screaming intensifying. Silas peeked out and saw a man running from a group of infected. The infected were *fast.* They easily caught up to him and delivered relentless blows with their fists that echoed like a butcher tenderizing meat. This horrific ordeal lasted for about fifteen minutes until the screaming ceased, but the pounding of their fists did not.

Another twenty minutes passed before a noise sounded in the distance, and the infected departed like a pack of wolves on the hunt.

Jesse looked at Silas. "Let's go, but be quiet."

They stood and continued forward.

Silas stayed on Jesse's tail as they proceeded for another block until they reached the building. It was an office building that had once housed a Texas bank, but the sign was broken, leaving only "OST NK TOER." Grunting and other eerie noises emanated from inside. They surveyed the area to ensure it was clear and then ran across the street.

Walking over broken glass, they carefully navigated the desolate building. Silas found the staircase, and up they went. With each floor they ascended, the infected's noises grew louder. They reached the eighteenth floor and slowly opened the door. Creeping along the office floor, they used the cubicles as cover. They walked toward the infected as thuds of fists sounded against the wooden walls. They soon reached the source, where they found four infected attempting to break into what appeared to be a manager's office.

"Aim for their heads," Jesse whispered. "If you can't, three shots to the chest should work."

Silas nodded.

"Be quick. Once we take them out, retrieve this woman and make a run for it because others will come."

He and Jesse carefully took aim at the infected. With a synchronized nod, they both opened fire. The gunshots echoed through the office, and within seconds, all four infected lay motionless on the floor, their unfeeling eyes staring into nothingness.

"Nice shooting," Jesse whispered as they cautiously approached the manager's office.

They carefully pushed the door open and found a young woman cowering in the corner, her eyes filled with terror.

"It's okay. We're here to help," he said, extending his hand to her.

She hesitated for a moment before taking his hand and standing.

"What's your name?" Silas asked gently.

"...Amelia."

He took a step back.

Jesse looked at him, puzzled.

"Amelia?" he asked, realization finally dawning on him. He hadn't recognized her in the dimly lit room and with her hair obscuring her face.

"Yes?" she responded, her voice tinged with uncertainty. "I was trying to get home to my little boy when I lost track of time. They chased me, and I just kept running. I somehow made it here."

They all walked toward the stairs but stopped when a startling growl reverberated. They turned to see that one of the four infected was missing.

Both Silas and Jesse raised their guns. Footsteps approached, growing louder. When the infected appeared in view, Silas started shooting, but his gun jammed. Jesse tried to shoot but missed. The infected tackled Silas with such force that they crashed into a nearby window, shattering it.

They fell, and all Silas saw was the night sky. The stars seemed to grow farther and farther away. It felt like an eternity before he hit the ground with a thud and a crack.

Everything went black.

The spinning and falling feeling returned. Silas then heard their voices. Jesse was talking about some movie he and Sandra had watched last night.

Silas slowly opened his eyes and adjusted to the room's bright light. He looked over and said, "The sequel is much better than the first movie."

Jesse and Amelia both spun around and laughed. They then helped him up and had him drink some water. As he was getting used to being back, he recounted what had happened on Earth 0001.

"So, I have a thought on this," Jesse said. "What I've noticed so far is that Jason King has always taken over or brought destruction to each world. Granted, we haven't been to all of them but still. Another thing is that either you or Amelia end up dying. It seems that for some reason, whenever we visit, one of you dies. But why? And what does that mean for our Earth?"

Amelia nodded. "I still feel like we should test a few more to confirm that. We might find a place that didn't fall under his power." She looked at the time. "If we rotate out, we may be able to finish world 007 today."

Jesse and Silas agreed.

12

The Twelfth Chapter: Unexpected

"You're absolutely right, Amelia," Silas said as they discussed their findings from The Echo Machine in their office the next day. "If Jason King gains access to the knowledge and technology from The Echo Machine, he could potentially explore and manipulate multiple worlds. It's a frightening thought—especially considering the destruction he's caused in the worlds we've encountered so far."

"We can't afford to underestimate him," Jesse said. "Our priority should be to protect our Earth and prevent him from causing any more harm. We need to find a way to stop him and to secure The Echo Machine before it falls into the wrong hands."

The weight of their mission hung heavy in the air as they realized the gravity of their situation. Time was of the essence, and they had to act swiftly.

"Let's bring Scarlet into this," Silas said. "She should be informed."

They both agreed.

"The thing is we need to find where he's hiding. I hate to say it, but convincing him to not continue won't be enough. We'll have to permanently stop him."

This wasn't the day they had hoped for, but it was a necessary task.

"I'll call her," Silas said.

Jesse handed him his phone, which had the secure messaging app.

He dialed her through the app. "Hey, Scarlet. It's Silas. We need to talk."

Silence lingered on the line for a moment.

"What's going on?" she asked. "What's wrong?"

"I can't discuss it over the phone. We need you here. I'll send you the address. Please get here as soon as you can."

"O-okay. I'll leave in a few minutes."

He ended the call, and they turned their attention to Jason's various destructive actions in different worlds. As they reviewed the evidence and discussed the gravity of the situation, they couldn't help but feel responsibility weigh on their shoulders.

"We have to be prepared for whatever comes our way," Jesse said. "We need to gather information, find his whereabouts, and develop a plan to stop him once and for all."

Amelia nodded. "Our world's safety and the safety of countless others are at stake."

Scarlet soon walked in and gave Amelia and Jesse a warm hug. Amelia then took her on a quick tour of the machine room, showing her the various machines. Including the original one that had brought them both success and pain—The Vale Machine.

While they were touring, Silas turned to Jesse. "I've thought about it as well," he said. "But I'm sure you and Amelia already know that the time line doesn't change. Just because I didn't die, it doesn't mean it will come back to correct what Jason stopped. We will never know when it might happen. But none of us know when it's our time to fulfill the contract we signed with death when we were born. What I do think is that Jason altering the time line by keeping me alive makes me nervous about what could happen."

Jesse patted his shoulder.

Amelia and Scarlet walked back into the room, carrying drinks for everyone. They all sat, and the trio explained everything to Scarlet. First, they discussed the basic functioning of the machine. They then delved into the various worlds they had visited. It took a few rounds of explanations for Scarlet to truly grasp the reality of the situation. Once she started to understand, they moved on to discuss the significance of the relationships between each world. They explained their fear that Jason King, her father, was on the same destructive path that had led to the total control and near-destruction of each planet they had visited.

They briefly touched on how the time line worked, emphasizing that they could alter the present to prevent a particular future, but there were certain aspects—like death—that couldn't be changed. They could only temporarily pause it as the natural flow of time would eventually correct itself.

All of this was a lot for Scarlet to absorb. She stood and paced the room, allowing everything to settle in her mind. After a few minutes, she returned to her seat. "So, what is your plan?"

"Well, we kind of waited for you to show up to work on that— since you are the one with the army," Amelia said. "Also, have you been able to track down your dad?"

"Not my dad. He will never be my dad. He's Jason King." She sighed. "But to answer your question, no. We think he's still in Washington but don't know exactly where. We have spotted his vehicles, but every time we get close, he manages to evade us. So, we must come up with a plan."

They all sat there for a while, discussing different ways to stop him.

"Does he still have his Control team?" Silas asked.

"As far as we know, he still has most of them," Scarlet replied, "which could be a couple hundred honestly. I mean, if we can find him, we can just kill him, right?"

The trio looked at each other.

"We don't think that would be a wise idea," Jesse said. "What we are also afraid of is if we kill him before he is supposed to die, what could happen to the time line."

Silence filled the room as they contemplated the potential consequences of taking such a drastic step.

Scarlet leaned back in her chair, deep in thought. "So, what do you suggest we do then?"

"We need a plan that could remove him from the equation," Amelia said. "Maybe we could lock him in jail or find a way to incapacitate him long enough to take him away somewhere. I don't know. Just tossing out ideas."

"I don't think the jail option is plausible," Silas said. "He's a former president, and no one will be able to convict him. I think the first step is to locate him. Maybe we could lure him out?"

"Jail won't be the right option," Scarlet said, "but how can we lure him out?"

They sat there, pondering what they could do.

"Silas," she said, and they all looked at her. "What if we use Silas to lure him out?"

"No!" Amelia responded.

She looked at her, shocked by the outburst.

"Sorry, but no. We will not use him. We don't know what he will do, and I don't think he cares about Silas anymore. Think about it. He knows where we are. What's stopping him from getting Silas now? Nothing. What would stop him from killing Silas if he does come out?"

Scarlet looked down. "I'm sorry I didn't..."

Amelia waved it off.

"We will figure something out to draw him out," Jesse said. "I—" His phone rang. He looked at it and then looked up with curious eyes.

"What's wrong? Is it Sandra?"

He shook his head. "It says it's you, Amelia. It says you're calling me."

She pulled her phone out of her pocket, but it just showed her home screen. She wasn't calling anyone.

"Should I answer it?"

Her phone buzzed. It was a text from Jesse that said "Yes, you should answer it. This concerns all of you."

She read the text out loud, and they all went silent, fearful of who it could be.

Jesse answered the phone and put it on speaker. "Hello?" he said.

The deep voice on the other end sent shivers down their spines. The caller spoke slowly and deliberately. "I know what you're planning. All of you."

Amelia's eyes widened, and she exchanged worried glances with the others.

"Who is this?" Jesse demanded. "How do you know what we're planning?"

Heavy breathing lingered on the other end of the call. "You know who I am, Jesse, Silas, Amelia, and Scarlet. You all tricked me into going to Louisiana rather than to Scarlet's home in Hot Springs."

"Captain Joel?" Jesse paused. "How do you know what we are planning?"

"Y'all forgot I have access to your phones. I kept that access after I was removed from my government position when Jason left office. It seems like Jason forgot I had that access as well. He tried to take me out, but I killed the potential murderer. I won't let him get away with that again.

"Y'all are right. He has no interest in Silas. But I have something that will lure him out. His paranoia has gotten the better of him. He's called his former overseas colleagues and friends and is calling in all his favors for funds, supplies, and people to build him a new machine."

They looked at each other.

"We figured he would be trying to build the machine again, but we are afraid he will try to build his version of The Echo Machine, which I'm sure you heard us talk about," Silas said. "But what is the thing you have that will lure him out of hiding?"

The captain didn't respond right away. All they heard was heavy breathing. "The one thing he cared about. Not as much as power but close enough. I had them shipped in last night."

He then texted a picture, which Jesse showed around the circle. It was of Sarah, Taylor, and Mary. Jason's family.

The captain continued. "I would say I'm sorry, Scarlet, but I'm not. This isn't business anymore. This is personal. He came after me and my wife. And I don't take well to people who come after the one person who brings me peace."

"Are you going to hurt my sisters and my mom?" Scarlet asked.

The captain sat in silence for a moment. "It depends on how

Jason acts but probably not. I will contact you soon with his location. If you're willing, we can work together."

The phone clicked, and the room was silent.

After the phone call, they sat there in silence.

"He was listening to us. Probably still is," Silas said. "Is he really going to side with us, or is he just using us?"

"Not much different from us," Scarlet said. "We use him for what he has, and he uses us for what we have."

They nodded except for Amelia.

"What do we have?" Amelia asked. "He could do this on his own, right? Unless...unless..." Worry etched across her face. "Unless he left the Control officers with him after Jason's attempted murder."

13

The Thirteenth Chapter: Clarity in Paranoia

The tapping of keys echoed throughout Jason's house, heightened by the sense of anticipation. He stood there, peering over the shoulder of an engineer who specialized in coding. The engineer was engrossed in reading the documents stolen from Silas, Jesse, and Amelia. He methodically flipped through various folders, opening each document and scanning through multiple pages to quickly absorb the contents.

As Jason loomed behind the man seated at the computer, his gaze remained focused on the documents displayed on the screen. Every line of code, each diagram, and all the scientific jargon filled his mind with a mixture of curiosity and suspicion.

The engineer, drenched in sweat from the fear of Jason's presence, worked diligently, clicking through the information before him. He could hear Jason's breathing and even his own heart pounding. Several hours had passed since he took his place in the chair. He found himself engaged in muttered conversations with himself, a desperate attempt to gain a better understanding of the complex material before him.

Jason's impatience grew. He leaned in, his eyes locked onto the engineer. "Well? Can you do it or not?" he asked, his tone laden with urgency.

The engineer continued to perspire profusely, anxiety evident under the weight of the former president's scrutiny. Thoughts raced through his mind, echoing the dire ultimatum Jason had given him earlier: answer him or he'd kill his son.

As the engineer's trembling hands navigated through the documentation, he glanced to his left, confronting the lifeless body of his colleague who had dared to oppose the former president's demands. Swallowing, he knew he had no choice but to comply.

He finally looked up at Jason and said, "Y-yes, sir, I-I can do this."

Jason responded with a triumphant clap of his hands, causing the engineer to flinch. He then slapped the engineer's shoulder. "Wonderful! See? That's all I ask. Why does everyone think I ask too much?" His tone was oddly nonchalant, as if the recent death was a trivial matter. He sighed. "That wasn't a question for you to answer. For you to not realize that makes me question your brilliance, but don't worry. As long as you know what you're doing, it's fine."

Only then did Jason shift his gaze down toward the deceased man. "Tsk, tsk, tsk. What a waste of a .45. Oh well." His eyes found the engineer's once more. "So, there's one more thing I want you to look at. It's called the Future Project. This is something I want you to focus on intensely because it may mean the difference between life and death. I hope your answer is better than your buddy's over there."

The engineer wiped the sweat from his eyes, knowing that if he didn't prove himself useful, he could end up like his unfortunate colleague. He clicked on the file and began to review it. It took him about an hour to read through and grasp the concept.

"This...this is different from what you had me look at before, Mr. President," the engineer said, his voice still trembling.

"Don't call me Mr. President. Just call me Mr. King. Besides, we're friends now, right?"

The engineer hesitantly nodded. "Yes, sir. But this is different. The way these things are written to run... It'll work on the same machine, but it doesn't seem to do the same thing. It appears to be..."

"Appears to be???" Jason said, growing impatient.

He looked back through the document. "The coding doesn't make sense. In order for me to better understand it and confirm what I think it is—which is groundbreaking—I need to test it."

Jason's face turned red, but he spoke calmly. "Okay. But you're not answering what the hell I just asked. What is it?"

He looked at him. "It seems that... Again, I'm not one hundred percent sure. But from how it's written, it appears to be a way to traverse parallel worlds, sir. See here?" He pointed toward some code on the document. "This is the code, and if you run it like this, it returns our coordinates. However, there are extra numbers at the end of each. Again, I don't know if I'm right, but I would like to test it out."

Jason laughed, his skepticism showing. "Another *universe?* Like the multiple worlds in the comics I read growing up? That can't be real."

He lightly chuckled. "That's what I'm reading, but if it is real, we need to thoroughly test this."

Jason stood there, observing the engineer closely. Despite the clear fear the engineer had of him, it became apparent that this engineer was telling the truth. "Okay. Well, let's get started. We don't have a lot of time."

Jason grabbed his phone and made some calls. While on the phone, he handed the engineer a list of supplies and instructed him to order them and to ensure the parts would arrive by tomorrow. He had somehow secured the old Boston facility, which still had many parts. After he finished with his calls, he turned back to the engineer.

"Get up. We're leaving," he said.

The engineer stood and followed him out of the house and into one of the waiting vehicles. They headed to the airport and flew to Boston on a colleague's private jet, a colleague to whom Jason had promised great wealth to once the machine was built. Although it was just a lie.

Upon their arrival in Boston, Jason and the engineer headed straight to the secured facility—a sprawling, isolated complex hidden away from prying eyes. A perfect place to conduct their secretive experiments. As they entered the facility, the engineer was shocked at how many people were already there.

"How did you get people here so quickly?" he asked Jason.

"Don't worry about that. I pulled a few favors from all over the world. Did you manage to order the parts we needed?"

He nodded.

"Good. Now get to work. I need this done in three days!"

Jason headed upstairs to the former manager's office, which he had outfitted for himself. He didn't trust anyone here nor anyone outside the facility. His paranoia had really kicked in, which he thought was fine because it helped him be a better planner for this. From the office, which had a window overlooking the area below, he observed these people scurrying around like ants, building and tapping away.

He really did see them like ants. Not humans. He could squish them with his thumb or burn them with a magnifying glass. They were *worthless* outside this facility.

Control officers had been spread throughout the building, on constant watch. He had whatever was left of them after Joel had abandoned them when he decided to run away. They patrolled the corridors, monitored the communications, and ensured that no one left the premises. A tight grip.

The next two days were a whirlwind of activity. The engineer and his team worked tirelessly, assembling and connecting various components. Barely sleeping, Jason was a constant presence, hovering over them and micromanaging every detail.

As the machine took shape, its complexity became apparent. The physicist on the team struggled to understand the intricacies of Silas, Jesse, and Amelia's design. He found himself pouring over their stolen documents, trying to decipher the equations and algorithms. It was a daunting task, but he was determined to prove himself to Jason.

When the final day arrived, the machine stood before them—a massive, imposing structure of wires, screens, and metal. It hummed with energy, almost overwhelming. The engineer and the physicist made the final adjustments, their faces tense.

While possessed by his ambition and paranoia, Jason stood before the machine. He was determined to make it work. "I want to test it."

The engineer looked at him with concern. "Well, we have some—"

"Are you not listening to me?" His voice grew more impatient. "Am I not making sense to you?"

The engineer took a step back, visibly flustered. "No, you are, sir. My apologies." He turned to the two individuals working on the machine and the computer. "Get it ready."

The team swiftly went to work, setting up the time and place for Jason's journey.

As preparations continued, Jason turned back to the engineer. "When I get back, the next test I want is the one we talked about. It better be ready."

With that said, he lay on the table, and the technicians connected him to the machine. They asked if he was ready, and he nodded. The machine produced loud noises and flashing lights, and then silence enveloped the room as the former president went under.

As he was under—sent approximately three hundred years in the past—the Control officers made sure the engineers followed his instructions diligently, sending them back to work. They meticulously examined the coding and documents related to the Future Project. They continued their efforts for hours. This extended period of absence allowed them ample time to analyze and decipher the complex code and necessary modifications. They estimated it would take another day or two to complete the modifications and conduct a successful test.

After fifteen hours, they heard a groan, and Jason sat up. Or tried to. The extended time in the machine had left him dizzy and disoriented.

"Did you drug me?!" he shouted. "Are you trying to kill me?!"

The engineer attempted to assist him in sitting up, but he pushed him away. "Sir, we didn't do anything you hadn't instructed us to do. You've been in the machine for approximately fifteen hours."

Jason turned to his Control officer for confirmation. The officer nodded, which eased his anxiety somewhat.

As his breath slowly returned to normal, he asked in a calmer tone, "Is it ready? Did you manage to get everything in order for the Future Project?"

The engineer nodded. "We only need two days: one for the modifications and another for testing to ensure that the code is compatible with the machine."

Although not entirely pleased with this time line, he realized there was little he could do to expedite the process.

14

The Fourteenth Chapter: Quandary

"Jesse, you don't have to go with us," Amelia said as her friend stood in front of the dry erase board that laid out their plan.

Their strategy involved surrounding the location they believed Jason would be at and using Joel as bait to draw him out of hiding. They believed Jason would not have Control officers present on site. After finalizing their plan, Scarlet had departed to track him down, hoping Joel might have some idea of his whereabouts.

"You have a wife and daughter to be with. Not us."

"Stop," Jesse said. "What kind of husband or father would I be if I didn't help prevent him from causing mass destruction?"

They argued about this for a while, but eventually, she gave in to his choice.

They knew that time was not on their side.

The next day, they loaded up Jesse's vehicle, dropped Lucy off with Jesse's wife and daughter, and hit the road. Scarlet had told them about a lead Joel had about a Boston facility. They didn't glean too much information, considering the new employees didn't want to betray their new boss, but it was a start. That left the trio with a daunting over twenty-six-hour drive ahead.

The road stretched on endlessly. As they rotated turns driving through the night and into the next day, their conversations shifted between the impending mission, their own concerns, and reminiscences of their past adventures. Despite the gravity of the situation, they managed to find some humor in their shared experiences. Yet with each mile they covered, their resolve grew stronger, knowing that the fate of this world depended on their success.

"Sir."

Standing by the window in his office, Jason glanced toward the Control officer who had spoken. He didn't want to hear him though, his eyes returning to their locked position on the machine and the team working on it.

"Sir. Captain Joel had reached out to me. He raised a lot of questions."

He snapped out of his hyperfocus. "*Joel?*" he spat.

"Yes, sir."

Jason turned away, heading toward his laptop. He checked Captain Joel's recent phone conversations and discovered that he had spoken to Silas, Amelia, Jesse, *and* Scarlet. He tapped into their old phone records to eavesdrop. They had shared that Scarlet would home first, while the trio would take Jesse's car to his destination.

They had a plan.

Fury coursed through his veins. He shoved past the Control officer and went down to the machine. The engineer was sitting there, preparing to implement the modifications required.

"You! Get me back in!" he demanded Jason.

Scared, the engineer fell out of his chair. "S-sir? Where and when? We are about to begin the mo-modifications."

"They're on their way! Get me onto Highway 40, going east. I must intercept them! Now!"

"B-but, but that's much more complicated than..."

Jason's face turned beet red, and the vein on his forehead looked ready to burst at any moment. "If you can't do it, I'll find someone else. I can *replace* you!"

"Okay, okay, okay. I'll try." He turned to his team. "Let's get Mr. King hooked up."

They plugged Jason in, and the engineer did his best to plug in a location on Highway 40. He hit the Enter key, and the machine's noises and lights sprang to life.

Darkness engulfed Jason, who spun for a moment. Then he wasn't. A horn blared.

His vision cleared, and he found himself on a highway. But where were *they*? He drove, scanning each passing car for any sign of them. Nothing. They must be behind him.

An idea struck him.

He spotted an 18-wheeler, accelerated as fast as he could to pull up alongside it, and swerved into its path, striking its front left side. That part of the 18-wheeler went over his car's hood before the back wheels crashed into his trunk, causing the massive truck to flip onto its side. Jason's car hit the left barrier, flipped onto its roof, and was crushed, sending sparks and body parts scattering.

Jason woke up back at the Boston facility and rejected any assistance, shoving the team aside. "No. No! I'm not done. Put me back in. But this time, place me in Dallas." He specified the neighborhood in Dallas he wanted to go to. "I don't care about my identity. Just set it for an hour from now! Do it!"

The engineer followed his instructions.

Jesse's vehicle had to slow down on the highway due to a massive traffic backup. The trio was soon in bumper-to-bumper traffic.

Silas looked at the map and saw that the traffic was backed up for a mile. "Looks like we're going to be here for a while."

Amelia sighed, clearly frustrated. "This is not what we need right now. Every minute counts."

Jesse nodded. "I hope Scarlet is making good progress back at the facility. We can't afford any more setbacks."

"Hey, check to see if there are any back roads we can take to get around this."

Jason woke up and found himself in a different body and in a random house. He looked around the bedroom and out the window. It struck him that he was on Jesse's street, a place he had been monitoring. Good. After a quick search of the house, he didn't find a gun, but he found a large knife in the kitchen instead.

As he turned to leave, a woman walked in. "Hey, honey. Um, where are you going with that?"

He just shoved her aside and walked out the door.

"What the hell, Samuel?!" she yelled after him.

He proceeded down the street, reading the house numbers. It didn't take long for him to find Jesse's house. "Bingo," he whispered. He could hear a little girl and a dog playing in the backyard. He walked up to the front door and knocked.

Sandra answered. "Hello? Can I help you?"

Without hesitation, he pushed his way inside.

"What the hell are you doing?! Get out!" she yelled, but he silenced her by hitting the back of her head with the blunt end of the knife.

She fell to the ground.

He quickly approached the curtains, ripped a tieback, and used it to bind her hands behind her back. He then made her sit on her knees.

"Sit there and shut up," he ordered.

She complied, and they waited in silence.

Jesse's daughter soon walked into the room to get a drink but sensed that something was wrong.

"Sit next to your mommy," Jason instructed her.

Confused, she did.

While keeping an eye on them, he searched for Sandra's phone, found it, and held the phone up to her face to unlock it. After taking a picture of both of them, he sent it to Jesse, adding a caption "You want them alive? Come home and save them."

The trio was still stuck in traffic, moving at a snail's pace. Cars surrounded them on all sides, making escape impossible.

Jesse's phone buzzed. He assumed it was a message from Sandra. Perhaps another photo of their daughter with Amelia. Probably even one with Lucy. He unlocked his phone, but when he saw the photo on the screen, his heart sank, and his hands trembled.

"Jesse? Is everything okay?" Amelia asked, her concern growing.

He remained silent, staring at the image. Tears welled in his eyes. But he fought to hold them back. "Son of a bitch!" he exclaimed, his voice quivering. "We need to turn around!"

Silas, still bewildered by the sudden turn of events, turned his head to face Jesse. "What? Are you serious?" he asked, his voice filled with concern and disbelief.

She leaned over and saw the picture. Her mouth dropped.

Her eyes searched around, trying to find a solution. "W–we're boxed in. What do we do?" She looked at the phone once more. "Call the number. Call and see what they want."

The atmosphere in the car became increasingly tense.

Jesse clicked the call button, his skin prickling and his face flushed. A nauseating feeling churned in his stomach.

"I have your wife and daughter, Jesse," the person on the other end said.

Filled with anger and worry, he struggled to find the right words. "I... L–let them go, you son of a bitch. They have nothing you want... How do you know my name?"

Silence lingered on the other end of the line. Silas and Amelia stared at him, awaiting a response from the mysterious caller.

"Don't worry. I won't hurt them yet," the person on the other end said. "You know, this whole time thing has become confusing. I'm from the past, but in your present now, and now my present is your present? I don't know. Nor do I care. So, what's it going to be, Jesse, Amelia, and Silas? Come save these two precious ladies, or come stop me at the facility?"

Jesse's heart pounded.

"Funny enough, you're stuck in traffic, aren't you? What a shame that man had to die. Now how are you going to save them? You're stuck in traffic, surrounded by dangerous vehicles. It'll take you forever to get to your house *or* to the facility. And I really don't have a lot of time. I want to check out that Future Project file my team has been working on. So, the choice is yours. Time is ticking."

With those chilling words, the call ended.

15

The Fifteenth Chapter: Deterrence

Jesse's car inched forward, unable to get out.

"What d-do we do?" Jesse said, terrified of losing his wife and daughter.

The trio sat there, mulling the situation over in their minds.

"Wait. I have an idea." Amelia pulled out her phone and made a call, briefly explaining the situation. She soon hung up.

Both of them stared at her.

"What?" Jesse asked.

"I called Scarlet," she replied. "She assured me that it will be taken care of. Sandra and your daughter will be fine. She's sending someone over to rescue them. She will call back once Jason is taken care of."

His tension eased slightly, but he remained anxious, his mind going over everything.

They inched forward in traffic.

"Hold on. Call her back now."

Confused, Amelia dialed Scarlet's number and handed him the phone.

"Scarlet, did they get there yet?" he asked urgently.

"No, not yet," Scarlet replied.

"Okay. I have a plan. Don't kill him. Tie him up and make sure he doesn't hurt himself. That way, he'll be stuck in that body. Then send my wife and daughter to my sister-in-law's place."

Scarlet stayed quiet for a moment. "That's a wonderful idea. Okay. Let me make the call. I'll contact you as soon as it's done." She then hung up.

"Excellent idea, Jesse!" Silas said. "This way, he can't contact the facility, and he will be stuck, plugged into the machine."

This brought a bit of joy to the group, especially since the end of the traffic was coming into view. As they inched closer to the scene of the accident, they saw the carnage caused by Jason. Jesse's guilt weighed heavily on him.

"I know you're nervous, Jesse, but I really believe that Scarlet's people can handle this," Amelia said.

"This is my fault," Jesse said, his voice filled with remorse. "I should've sent them away. But I was too wrapped up in this. You were right. I should've stayed home. If they are harmed or...or worse, I don't know what I would do. They are my everything."

She leaned forward, wrapping her arms around him. "This isn't your fault. And everything will work out fine. They will be saved, and this will all be over."

Silas added his support by placing his hand on Jesse's shoulder.

Finally, they made it out of the traffic jam and were back on course. Jesse couldn't keep his eyes from glancing at his phone, anxiously awaiting the incoming call.

Jason paced back and forth in Jesse's living room, constantly checking the window. He didn't exactly know what he was looking for, but his paranoia made him feel as though someone was coming for him.

"What do you want with my husband?" Sandra asked, concern in her voice. "Are you part of that cult? He made peace with them."

He shot her a glance but continued pacing. "He knows what I want. He and his minions stopped me once before. Now it's my turn to stop him."

Sandra realized the connection. "You...you are the reason they're on this mission, Jason," she said.

He didn't respond, just continued to look at her.

"You really think this will stop him? Are you getting some sort of thrill from having power in this situation? What is your end goal? To rule the world? You can't even keep your *family* with you. What a small man you are."

Jason became infuriated. "You don't know what you're talking about! Don't talk to me like you know who I am or like you're better than me. You are nothing. *Worthless*. And don't talk to me about losing your family. Why isn't your husband here to protect you from me, the big bad man?"

She couldn't help but laugh at his arrogance. "You think you're better than my husband because he isn't here to protect me? Oh, you're very wrong about that. He is protecting us. He's on his way to stop you, you fool. What's sad is that I feel sorry for you. Lost your power. Removed from your office. Lost your family. All gone. You have nothing now. Did you even fight for your family? Probably not. You'd rather waste your time threatening me and my daughter than to fight for your wife and daughters to come back."

He grabbed dishes from the counter and hurled them at the walls, smashing them into pieces. "I *will* win them back. Once I regain control and expand my power all over the world, they'll *want* to come back. Just wait. You'll see. You'll also regret annoying me with your taunts. I hope you enjoy being a widow, and I hope your daughter enjoys life without a father. But don't worry. I'll pay for the funeral, and I'll be there to witness you two *weeping*, while I run this world with my wife and daughters."

Sandra, tied up by her daughter, did not show an ounce of fear. Instead, her face hardened. She aimed to fill his head with self-doubt and anger. To throw him off his plan.

She watched as Jason checked the windows once more. "Expecting someone?"

He didn't respond.

The power of being a mother was evident in her calm voice. "You're right to be nervous. I would be in your shoes."

He looked at her. "Shut up! You don't know anything. You don't know what I have planned. You don't know if he's coming or not. But I know. He can't come. He won't make it. He won't make it on *time*. And even if—by some miracle—he does, don't worry. I hold true to my word. You'll become a widow."

Sandra scanned the room, looking for a way to escape or take him down.

As time went on, he grew increasingly angry, smashing more items in fits of rage and paranoia. He grabbed her phone once more. "Let's see if this will make him hurry up." He opened the text message app and then the camera, grabbed a knife, and snatched her daughter.

Her daughter screamed, crying.

"NO! Stop!" she demanded. "She hasn't done anything! Use me! Don't touch her, you fucking asshole! You weak ass man! Pathetic piece of shit! Let her go!"

He grabbed her daughter by the back of her neck, pulled her in close, and held the knife to her throat. Tears fell from her beat red face. He took a quick photo of him holding the knife. Afterward, he lowered the knife and shoved her toward her mother. She landed on top of her.

"You really are a sick son of a bitch!" Sandra yelled. "I hope you don't die. I hope you suffer. I hope they torture you!"

He ignored her, leaning up against the counter and typing out a message to Jesse.

The front door swung open with a loud thud, and Katherine entered, brandishing a Colt Army Model 1860. She was elegantly dressed in a green sequin dress. "Get on the floor, you fool," Katherine declared, not mincing her words.

Shocked, Jason froze. But at least he had already hit send. His eyes darted between Katherine and Sandra and the little girl.

"Don't do it," Sandra said.

Despite the warning, he ran toward the mother and daughter. Katherine fired. The bullet struck his hand that held the knife, causing it to fly out of his hand and land on a nearby chair.

He fell to his knees, writhing. "What the hell!"

Katherine strutted over to him and kicked his stomach. From her dress, she produced several zip ties and bound his hands and feet together. She then walked over and untied Sandra. "You're okay now. Jesse, Amelia, and Silas called Scarlet, who sent me to save you." She then took off her wide-brimmed dark green hat, which had a yellow rose attached to it, and bent down to the little girl. "Hello, sweetie. You're okay now. Auntie Katherine is here." She placed the hat on the young girl, who smiled.

"This is very pretty, ma'am," the young girl said.

She smiled back, winked, and turned to Sandra. "Do you have a first aid kit? We need to prevent him from bleeding out."

Sandra nodded, fetched a first aid kit, and handed it to her. Katherine tended to his hand as he twisted and cursed, trying to escape.

"Now, sir, don't be so angry," Katherine said. "You'll heal up just fine. And don't use that nasty language in front of a little princess like that." She glanced at Sandra. "Call your husband and let him know you're okay."

Sandra called Jesse, who picked up fast. Yet he yelled into the phone, using all kinds of foul language. It sounded as if he was crying.

"Jesse, honey," she said, cutting him off and crying herself. "We are okay. Katherine saved us, and we have Jason tied up on the floor. We are okay."

He calmed down after a few more reassurances that they were okay. "We're still on our way," he muttered, his voice much lower now. "Keep him tied up. And make sure Katherine watches him. We need him to stay there."

She nodded. "We will. I love you so much." She then hung up and informed Katherine about what he had said.

Katherine hugged Sandra. "Everything will be okay now. But we can't stop. The end isn't here yet, but it's on the horizon."

She nodded once more.

Katherine lifted Jason's head and placed a rag in his mouth to silence him. She then turned to the mother and daughter. "You two, sit. I'll make some tea." She pulled out a pot, heated up some water, and retrieved a few tea bags of her favorite blend from her dress.

Sandra sat there, thinking she must have everything she needed in there. Which made her chuckle a little.

Katherine brought the tea over and added a little honey. "This will help calm the nerves. Plus, it's like we're having a tea party after taking down the big, bad guy." She winked at her daughter.

They sat there and sipped the tea. Sandra noticed it did indeed calm her nerves, causing her trembling hands to slow.

She repeated to herself that Jesse would get there in time. Jesse should get there in time...

16

The Sixteenth Chapter: UnPlugged

People bustled throughout the Boston building, trying to get the computers ready for the president to use the machine for the Future Project—when he got back. Jason had been in the machine for quite some time now, and one of the Control officers, who used to be Joel's second-in-command, was becoming weary that he had been in there for too long.

He walked up to the man Jason had put in charge of the project. "You! What's your name?"

The engineer turned around and saw the brooding man standing there. "My name? Um, yes. My name is Jim, which is short for Jimothy. My parents thought it was a funny name to give me."

"I didn't ask for your *backstory* on your name. I came over here to see why it's taking Mr. King so long. He should be out by now, right?"

Jimothy looked over at the machine. It *had* been quite some time. But he didn't care. That only gave him more time. "Well, Mr. Officer, the thing is, um, well, there's no telling what he could be doing, right? So, um, we have to wait for him."

"Well, we need him back. We need to pull him out."

He thought it over. "Well, sir, we can't. We don't know if something bad could happen to him. Worst-case scenario, he dies, and I won't be the cause of that."

Frustrated, the officer narrowed his eyes at him. "Well, we need him back. The cult and the three are on their way. What if something happened, and he can't get himself back here?"

"Well, I don't know. We don't really know how this works. The only ones who really know are the three we stole this information from."

"Well, I'll give him another hour. Give *you* another hour. If he isn't unplugged by then or if he doesn't come out of it, I'll do it myself." The officer turned and walked away.

Jimothy, now worried for his life and the others around him, stood frozen, wondering what would happen if they did unplug him early. He anxiously watched the machine, his mind racing. What were the potential consequences of forcing Jason out of the machine prematurely? He knew meddling with such advanced technology, which he didn't fully understand, could lead to what he theorized as a catastrophic outcome—not just for Jason's life but for the entire world.

As the minutes ticked away, he couldn't help but wonder if there was another way to handle the situation. He walked around, engaging with the other engineers and scientists to get their thoughts on it. He explained the predicament and sought their guidance, desperately hoping for a solution that would avoid any irreversible damage. But they had none.

The time drew closer to the end of the hour, and Jimothy could see the officer was growing impatient.

The officer soon walked up to him. "Have you figured it out yet?"

Jimothy shook his head.

"Well, you really are useless."

The officer walked toward the machine. "Come here, Jim."

Jimothy ran over to the officer.

"Do it. Unplug him. Now."

He stood there, confused about what to do.

"Do it, or you're dead!"

Sweat built along his forehead.

The officer pulled out his gun and pressed it against his forehead. "Do it!"

Jimothy slowly nodded and grabbed his computer. He began the shutdown process as if he were powering the machine down, moving through each step meticulously. He walked over to the machine, took a deep breath, and initiated its shutdown process.

Jason's heart rate began to increase rapidly.

He looked over at him, and his panic mounted.

"Don't stop!" the officer snapped.

He quickly flipped the last switch, completing the shutdown. He then looked over at the machine—only to stare at Jason's lifeless body. No movement. No heartbeat.

Nothing.

"Well?" the officer impatiently asked.

Just then, Jason seized. Jimothy quickly turned him on his side, removed the headband, and inserted an object into his mouth to prevent him from biting his tongue. After a few terrifying minutes, his seizures stopped, and his heart ceased to beat. Jimothy began administering CPR, desperately working to bring him back from the brink of death.

Eventually, his breath came back, but he remained unconscious.

"Is he okay?" the officer asked.

Jimothy nodded.

He stood there, watching over Jason. Waiting to see if he woke up. So was the officer. No one moved an inch. No one made a single noise. Only the officer's watch ticked, its sound echoing throughout the room. Then there was a cough. Jason stirred.

"Sir, you're awake," the officer said.

Jason slowly opened his eyes and looked around, confused. His vision was hazy at first, and the room's harsh fluorescent lights made him squint. He tried to move, but a dull ache pounded throughout his body. Panic crept in as he struggled to remember what had happened. Fragments of memories began to surface—the machine, the shutdown process, and the excruciating pain.

Jimothy watched him closely, his anxiety mounting. "Sir... can you hear me?" he asked cautiously.

His gaze settled on Jimothy, and a mixture of fear and anger crossed his face. He tried to sit up but winced, causing Jimothy to rush to his side to help.

The officer, still tense, inquired, "What happened in there? Do you remember anything?"

Jason froze, sitting there as more memories flooded his mind. "Yes... I remember being tied up and then intense pain... The most intense pain I've ever experienced. Then it all went black, and I'm back here."

Jimothy hesitated, exchanging a nervous glance with the officer. "You're correct. You are at the Boston facility, sir."

He slowly started sitting up, but his head spun, and his legs felt like they were asleep. Jimothy tried to help him into a sitting position, yet he shoved him away. "What did you do?!"

"Um, sir, well, we were worried about how long you were under. I was informed to bring you back, even though I didn't want to in fear of disrupting the universe or killing you."

Jason's anger flared as he tried to regain his bearings. "You could have killed me!" he barked, his voice a mixture of frustration and fury.

"I–I'm really sorry, sir. We didn't know what else to d–do. It seemed like you were in there for too long, and we were concerned."

He calmed his nerves some and glared at Jimothy. "Okay... Well, I'm glad you got me out because I was tied up, and they wouldn't let me come back. But hell, that *hurt*."

Jimothy, still not knowing how to read Jason's reactions, hesitated.

"What's the status of the machine? Is it operational? Can we proceed with the Future Project?"

He hesitated for a moment more before responding, "Y–yes... The coding is ready. We just need to make a few adjustments to the machine before proceeding. We were waiting for your return to start the final settings."

Jason clenched his jaw, frustrated by the delay but knowing he couldn't afford to make rash decisions. "*Fine*. Make the adjustments. But we don't have much time."

17

The Seventeen Chapter: Arrival

After many hours and crossing numerous state lines, the trio finally arrived in Boston. Exhausted but determined to put an end to all of this, they knew they couldn't stop. Jesse called Scarlet to give her the update that they were about thirty minutes away. She informed him that they were about to leave their Boston safe house. She also mentioned that Joel would be meeting them there. All of which he relayed to the other two in the car.

The Boston cityscape unfolded before them. The sun began to dip below the horizon, casting long shadows over the road ahead. The trio knew the hours of darkness would be their ally in this dangerous endeavor.

Renewed energy surged within Jesse, Amelia, and Silas. They knew that the fate of not just their world—but countless others—rested on their shoulders.

"Whatever happens today, I love both of you, okay?" Amelia said.

Silas and Jesse exchanged glances before looking back at her.

"Nothing bad will happen like last time," Silas said. "We are better prepared, and Jason is unstable."

Jesse nodded.

This brought some comfort to her. She couldn't bear the thought of losing Silas again.

As they got closer, about a block away from the facility's entrance, they encountered a line of vehicles. Scarlet stood outside one, engaged in conversation with another person. They pulled up next to her.

"So, this is it, huh?" Amelia said out the window.

Scarlet nodded. "Yeah. Go park over there, and we'll head up. Joel said he's arriving soon. Hopefully, we can talk to Jason and convince him to change his mind. If anything, maybe we can avoid shedding blood this time."

They drove around the corner and parked the car. All three got out and joined Scarlet.

"The original plan is to enter the facility, take control, and reason with Jason," Scarlet said. "We'll use his family as leverage if necessary. If that doesn't work, Joel mentioned using his family against him, whatever that entails. If all else fails, we'll have to resort to force. But remember, we can't kill him."

She pointed at a map, designating team leaders for each group and providing instructions on where to enter. Her group was to enter through the front while two other teams were to approach from the back. With a predetermined signal, they would enter the building and execute the initial plan, adjusting it as needed.

Amelia listened with a mixture of determination and anxiety. She exchanged glances with Silas and Jesse, silently reaffirming their commitment to see this through. With the plan outlined, they all adjusted their equipment, checked their communications, and took a deep breath. Silas grabbed his laptop and tools, ready to face the uncertain future that awaited them.

The trio shared a final moment of peace before setting out to confront the man who had caused so much chaos in their lives.

As Scarlet and the trio walked toward the facility, Silas's palms sweated, and Amelia's heart raced. In contrast, Jesse remained calm. He knew he had to do this for his family. It was his mission to take Jason down personally.

They approached the imposing facility's entrance, where two guards were stationed.

"The time has come," Scarlet muttered.

They walked up to the guards, who promptly pulled out their weapons.

"You need to leave!" a guard ordered.

She let out a mocking laugh. "Get out of my way, or I'll be stepping over you."

The guards exchanged glances and chuckled. She raised both hands, forming finger guns, and repeated her threat. Once more, they laughed. However, a gunshot echoed from the distance, and one guard dropped to the ground. She lowered her left hand, and the second guard, now bewildered, held up his weapon.

"Get on the ground!" he demanded.

Amelia, Silas, and Jesse exchanged glances.

"Leave or move!" Amelia said. "Or you'll be lying next to your friend!"

The second guard didn't move.

Another shot from the distance echoed. The second guard was hit, falling onto the ground.

She turned around to the trio and chuckled. "I did warn them, did I not?"

With the guards incapacitated, she signaled for her team to move forward. They proceeded through the gate and into the facility's compound, the tension thick. They walked down the long road that led to the building, while the two teams in the back informed her that they had made it over the wall and were closing in on the building.

Silas felt his anxiety rise. Amelia grabbed his hand and then reached for Jesse's. Together, they walked behind Scarlet.

So far, they hadn't encountered any more guards.

Near the building's entrance, they stopped, taking cover behind some bushes. Two guards stood by the front door. Scarlet contacted the individual who had taken out the other two guards, instructing them to handle these as well. After a few seconds, a sharp crack rang, and one guard fell. The second guard reached for his radio, but before he could make the call, another shot echoed, and he too was down.

As they continued to scope out the area, a vehicle approached. They quickly ducked behind cover by the road. A large black SUV pulled up to them and came to a stop. The window rolled down, revealing Joel inside.

"Ready?" he asked.

Scarlet nodded.

They stood and followed his vehicle to the entrance. At the front, he got out of the vehicle but left it running.

Scarlet walked up to him.

"You all should go in and do what you need to," he said. "I'll be here with his family."

She nodded.

Several Control officers walked out with their guns raised.

"DON'T MOVE!" one shouted.

The whole group froze in their tracks.

After a moment, Joel took a step forward. "Gentlemen, lower your weapons. We're here to talk to Jason. That's it."

However, they did not lower their weapons. Instead, they took a step closer. Then another. Amelia, Jesse, and Silas looked at each other, still holding each other's hands. The Control officers' fingers rested near the trigger, and they wore stern expressions. The standoff continued for a few moments, neither side willing to make the first move.

"Hold on there, gentlemen," a familiar voice echoed from behind the Control officers, a tone oozing with a mixture of arrogance and curiosity. Jason King emerged from the shadows of the building, flanked by several loyal guards. "Let them through."

The Control officers reluctantly lowered their weapons, their stern expressions replaced with uncertainty.

He approached the group, eyeing them with a calculating gaze. "Well, well, well... What brings you all to my doorstep today?"

Scarlet stepped forward, determination in her eyes. "We're here to talk. To find a peaceful solution."

He chuckled, his lips curling into a sly grin. "Peaceful, you say? You always were the optimistic one, Scarlet. Very well. Let's talk. But remember, I hold all the cards here."

"You're right, Jason," Jesse said. "You hold all the cards here. That is why we are here to reach a peaceful resolution. We have seen what will happen and what has happened in other worlds. So far, all we've witnessed is death and destruction. We don't want that. And we know you don't want that."

Jason looked at them, studying their bodies. "Death and destruction, huh? Well, here's the thing. Why do you assume I don't want that?" His face contorted with anger. "Of course, I don't want that, but sometimes, for the betterment of what I want, I'm willing to sacrifice others to get it."

Scarlet took a step closer, her voice unwavering. "You really are wrapped up in your own world. You think just because you want something means you deserve it. Here's the thing, Jason: your life means *nothing* to the thousands who could die because of the power you want."

A vein in Jason's forehead pulsated.

"If you come to peace with us, that—*that*—is a great power," Jesse said. "Being able to give up what you desire for others takes tremendous power."

He rolled his eyes. "You talk to me about power, yet you couldn't even come save your wife and child. You had someone else do your dirty work for you, you pathetic little man."

Jesse's anger rose, but Amelia's grip on his hand reminded him of their mission. "At least I still have my family," he replied with cold determination. "I didn't lose mine because my ego pushed them away. I didn't shoot my daughter and wife."

Jason's anger bubbled, but he laughed. "You have *no clue* what you're talking about. I sent them away to keep them safe while I tried to get your machines working again after your pathetic attempt to stop me last time," he said, slightly lying.

Joel chuckled. "Oh, Jason. *You* don't even know what you're talking about. Sending them away? That's a lie. They ran away. They hid from you. You became the monster they feared. I know I'm a monster. I know I do horrible things. But I don't lie about my family."

"Oh, is that so, Joel?"

"Yes," he said calmly. "So, let's end this peacefully."

Jason laughed again. "There will be no peace. What can you do to stop me? Nothing. I know about the people waiting for your order, Scarlet. They're hiding behind the building. I didn't care about the guards out by the gate. Why? Because they weren't actual guards. I put two scientists in control uniforms. The same goes for in front of the building's entrance. They meant nothing to me."

Joel sighed. "Well, if there won't be peace, and you truly don't care..." He walked over to the SUV, opened the back door, grabbed Mary—one of Jason's twins. He dragged her to the front of the car, in view of Jason. "Let's go over this again, Jason. You don't care who dies, right? So, you don't care about her." Joel pulled out his pistol.

Tears built in the child's eyes.

Amelia, Jesse, and Silas looked on with wide eyes, their hearts pounding. Scarlet's expression turned cold, and she tightened her grip on her weapon.

Jason's face contorted, showing a fleeting sign of fear before reverting to anger. He laughed. Again. Loudly. "What, Joel? You're going to hurt a little girl? You think hurting my daughter will stop me?"

Joel maintained a stern look, unwavering. "Oh, but here's the thing, Jason. I can. I will do whatever it takes to stop you. You started all this. You came after me because of *your* paranoia."

Tears streamed down Mary's face. "Daddy, please don't let him hurt me."

Jason's anger flared. "You brought them here to threaten *me*? Who's the bad guy *now*? Me? I'm here to make the world better, to make it better for me. You're the one with the gun pointed at my daughter."

Joel didn't answer. Instead, he loaded a round into his pistol, his determination unwavering. "This is your last chance, Jason."

Screams and cries emanated from inside the car. All eyes were locked on Joel.

Jason's panic intensified, his anger growing. "Stop!"

But it was too late. Joel's finger tightened on the trigger, and a gunshot rang out. Followed by a thud on the ground.

The gunshot echoed through the tense air. Silence fell upon the group.

Mary lay on the ground, her small body trembling but miraculously unharmed. She clutched her chest, where a bulletproof vest had absorbed the shot.

Joel had fired a warning shot.

Jason's face paled as he realized he had been outmaneuvered. This anger consumed him even more. "Raise your guns!" he yelled to the Control officers, who listened.

Joel pointed the pistol toward Mary's head, his face turning red. "I won't miss, Jason. I won't miss." A bead of sweat rolled down his forehead.

"Fine... You win," Jason said.

"Get over here then."

He stood there, his mind racing as he tried to think of a way out of this situation. His eyes darted to each person present, but his paranoia only intensified.

Joel, becoming impatient, said, "Hurry up, Jason. Don't stall. I'm going to start counting."

He looked around, still trying to come up with a plan.

"Five."

Panic gripped him.

"Four."

Amelia didn't blink. Instead, she squeezed both Jesse's and Silas's hands.

"Three."

Scarlet's eyes darted between Joel and Jason.

"Two."

The Control officers remained motionless, their fingers hovering above the triggers as they aimed at all of them.

"One," Joel said, his voice stern.

"Don't let them in!" Jason shouted.

Before he could do anything else, Joel made eye contact with Jason and fired a gunshot. Jason's face dropped as he looked down at his daughter, who was still unhurt. His eyes then found his shoulder, which was now bleeding.

Without hesitation, Jason rushed inside and closed the door behind him.

In a split second, Joel grabbed Mary, while Silas, Scarlet, Jesse, and Amelia ducked behind cover just as the Control officers opened fire.

18

The Eighteen Chapter: Cease

As Silas, Scarlet, Jesse, and Amelia crouched behind cover, a cacophony of bullets whizzed past. The sharp impacts against rock and steel filled the air. All too chaotic.

Nearby, Joel managed to usher Mary back into the vehicle. Rounds hit the vehicle's doors, and the glass shattered. He climbed into the driver's seat, put the vehicle into drive, and executed a U-turn. The vehicle's wheels spun, screeching, until he took off, never to be seen again.

Silas, Amelia, Jesse, and Scarlet simply watched as he sped into the distance.

Yet then Scarlet, with a swift assessment of the situation, took charge. She communicated with the snipers, directing them to provide covering fire. With a calm demeanor, she initiated contact with the group stationed at the building's rear, urging them to prepare for entry.

She gripped her pistol, her senses honed. Peering over her cover, she took precise shots, neutralizing two officers with lethal accuracy. Her sniper skillfully eliminated the remaining threats.

With the gunfire ceased, the team wasted no time. She signaled to the rear group, instructing them to advance. The air was thick as they stood on the brink of entering the heart of the chaos, where Jason still lurked.

Turning to the three companions by her side, Scarlet spoke, her voice steady but empathetic. "Are you ready?"

Nervousness lingered in their expressions, but they nodded. With a determined nod back, she swung the door wide open, revealing the pandemonium inside the building.

Jason's enraged voice echoed orders through the corridors. Control members swiveled their weapons, first pointing at the bewildered employees and then redirecting their aim toward the approaching cult members. The scene was a frantic mix of shouting, fear, and tension. Employees scurried about, trying to comply with Jason's orders, while the Control officers pushed forward, trying to navigate through the chaos without causing any unnecessary harm.

"Kill anyone who isn't doing something!" he yelled.

As the four traversed the chaos, another gunshot rang. Then another. Along with more screaming.

"We need to get this over with!" Scarlet said.

"Kill all who don't belong here!" he screamed before running to his office.

The Control officers opened fire, but so did the cult members. Gunfire and the hissing of bullets filled the air, mingling with screams.

Jesse, fueled with anger for what Jason had put his wife and daughter through, sprinted after Jason before the office door closed.

"JESSE!" Amelia yelled.

But he didn't stop. He made it up the steps and burst through the door, yelling, "Where the hell are you?!"

Jason appeared out of nowhere, swinging his fists. He struck Jesse's chin and knocked him over, repeatedly landing blows. But Jesse was too consumed by anger to feel the pain. Instead, Jesse managed to push him off and delivered a powerful kick to his stomach, causing him to exhale a painful burst of air. Jesse then attempted to kick his face, but he blocked the kick, which threw Jesse off balance and gave him enough time to regain his footing.

Amid the chaos of their fierce struggle, the room seemed to shrink. The walls closed in as if echoing the intensity of their conflict.

Jason's adrenaline-fueled instincts kicked in as he ducked beneath Jesse's wild punch, narrowly avoiding the blow. With swift agility, he countered that by launching a lightning-quick jab toward Jesse's midsection.

Jesse, his anger still raging like a storm, managed to twist out of the way just in time. His heart pounded in his chest, his chin throbbing.

Their breaths came in ragged gasps.

With a sudden surge of energy, Jesse lunged forward. The two adversaries were locked in a fierce embrace, each trying to gain the upper hand. Their combined weight sent them crashing into a nearby table, shattering it into pieces.

Desperation fueled their movements as they grappled on the floor, trying to gain some leverage. Furniture and office supplies scattered and shattered in the chaos. Blood trickled from Jesse's lip, mixing with the sweat that coated his face, but he barely noticed the pain.

The two men raged on. Jason, fueled by desperation, threw punches with wild abandon, while Jesse, driven by his rage, threw punches with fierce resolve. Their faces bore the marks of their brutal brawl. They continued to fight—exhausted, out of breath, and in pain.

Jesse went for another blow to Jason's face, but he missed, causing him to stumble. Jason grabbed him and pushed him out the door and against the railing. He still swung, hitting Jason once more. Jason grabbed his collar with one hand and punched him with the other. Blow after blow to the face left Jesse only able to see out one eye.

"Your family will be joining you soon," Jason said menacingly. He pushed Jesse over the ledge.

Jesse fell, landing on the hard concrete floor and breaking his neck.

The room went silent from the thud. Except for a single gasp.

It was Amelia who had gasped. She had heard the thud and turned to see Jesse motionless on the cold concrete floor. As she stared at his motionless body, her heart felt like it had stopped. Tears welled in her eyes, and a mixture of grief and anger overwhelmed her.

Silas and Scarlet, realizing what had just happened, turned their attention to Jason.

The chaos around them continued as the battle between the Control officers and the cult members raged on.

"We have to continue," Scarlet said.

Silas and Amelia looked at each other, their faces reflecting both rage and misery. They wanted to put an end to Jason, but Scarlet was right. They had to stay focused on their mission to prevent further destruction and loss. With heavy hearts, they resumed their work, determined to reach the machine.

Scarlet led the way with her gun ready, while Silas and Amelia followed closely behind. They cautiously moved through the tumultuous scene, keeping an eye on the remaining Control officers and cult members. Sporadic gunshots and shouts echoed from various corners. The chaos around them was disorienting.

Yet when they reached the machine, someone was already working on it.

"No!" Jimothy said. "You can't do this!"

"We have to," Silas replied. "We must stop him from using the machine. He will cause more death than what he has already caused."

He hesitated—but then stepped aside.

Silas and Amelia dismantled the machine, tearing it down piece by piece. Scarlet held her gun up at the ready, doing her best to protect them from any approaching Control officers. In the distance, Jason's frantic cries echoed.

"NO! NO! NO!"

They exchanged determined glances and accelerated their efforts. Amelia turned to work on the computer as well—to erase all data related to the machine.

In the office window that overlooked the area, Jason appeared with a pistol. He lifted the gun and fired a shot that struck Scarlet in the face, tearing through her cheek and bringing her down with a scream of agony.

Silas and Amelia quickly turned around, witnessing the horrifying scene.

"No!" Silas looked up in shock. "Hurry, Amelia!"

Jason raised the weapon once more and fired another round, hitting her shoulder. The searing pain caused her to scream out.

"Keep going!" Silas called.

His laughter echoed throughout the room. He lifted his weapon again and fired, striking Silas this time. Silas slumped against the machine and then slid off. He then lay motionless on the floor.

She let out a bloodcurdling scream. Her gaze slowly turned to Jason. Anger and pain seeped from her voice. "*YOU!*"

Amelia spotted Scarlet's fallen pistol nearby, grabbed it with her good hand, and took off running. She ascended the steps and ran down the hall—toward Jason. Raising the pistol, she fired three shots in rapid succession. One hit his shoulder, another struck his knee, and a third hit the shin of his other leg, causing him to collapse.

She stumbled up to him. "You sick sadistic asshole!" she screamed, tears streaming down her face. "You will not live to see another day! You will rot in hell!" She lifted the pistol to his head, her hand shaking. Her lip quivered.

A gunshot rang out.

Amelia stood there, shock filling her face. She dropped the pistol and touched her chest. It was warm and wet. Blood covered her hands.

"You're such a fool, thinking you can get away with this," Jason snapped. "I hope you enjoy being with your friends."

She took a step back, staggering. Tears streamed down her face. She fell onto her back, her vision becoming blurry. She lost feeling in her legs and arms, and her breathing became harder. "I'm coming for you, Silas," she whispered.

Her vision went black.

19

The Nineteenth Chapter: E-0007

Silence, darkness, weightlessness—nothing. There was nothing. No pain. No sadness. No happiness. Nothing. A void, a space devoid of sensation or consciousness. Time seemed to lose its meaning, stretching into an eternity of nothingness. It was as if existence itself had paused, suspended in a state of profound emptiness.

From a distance, there was tapping.

The tapping echoed throughout the space, a constant rhythm of tap, tap, tap. Waves of light formed from the taps and the echoes of the taps. These waves pulsed with increasing intensity. The once-empty void quivered as if it was waking from a long slumber.

As the waves of light strengthened, they took on colors that defied description. Brilliant hues that had never been seen before danced across the void, creating a mesmerizing display of spectral beauty. The darkness slowly pushed back, revealing hints of form and substance.

Amid this evolving kaleidoscope of colors, faint whispers emerged. They were like distant voices—soft and unintelligible at first but gradually gained clarity. Though still unintelligible.

The tapping continued, now accompanied by the rhythmic hum of ancient, powerful stirring. Shapes and contours emerged from the swirling colors, forming into ethereal structures. As if a new reality was being born out of a void. Each moment giving birth to something more intricate and wondrous than the last.

As the whispers grew louder, and the light became more intense, a sense of purpose and meaning filled the once-empty space. Existence was no longer suspended but was finding its own path forward. A cosmic awakening. A rebirth of consciousness in a realm where none had existed before. The void had transformed into a canvas.

The tapping continued, now soothing.

Then silence again. Followed by a blinding light.

"Stay with us!" a voice from the distance said.

"Don't go!" another voice said.

Floating in the nothingness, uncertainty filled the void.

The pleas grew more desperate, urging the consciousness to stay. To resist the allure of the light. But the allure was undeniable, and the need for answers pushed the thoughts forward.

With each passing moment, the light seemed to grow closer, more intense. As if it was pulling the consciousness toward it. The choice between the familiar comfort of the tapping and the enigmatic promise of the light hung.

The light became so bright.

As she opened her eyes, everything appeared blurry with figures surrounding her. One person was sitting on her, pressing their hands down on her chest and then lifting them. She blinked a few more times. It was Silas. Sitting on her. Giving her chest compressions.

"JESSE, SHE'S AWAKE!" Silas yelled. He bent over, hugged her tightly, sat her back down, and got off her. "Amelia, can you hear me?"

She looked around. They were back in the facility in Dallas.

"Can you hear me?"

She looked at him and nodded. "What... Where... Why are we here? We were in Boston, right?"

Jesse ran over to her with a smile. "Oh, thank goodness you're alive. We thought we lost you."

She looked around once more. "What happened?"

He and Silas both looked at each other.

"Don't you remember?" Silas asked.

She shook her head, her head pounding.

"After I got back from Jason's clutches, you let me use the machine. We then agreed to test out our theory of Jason taking over the other worlds. You agreed to go to 0007. You've been under for about eighteen hours now, Amelia," he said, concerned.

"What do you *mean*?" she snapped. "Are you saying that we didn't try to stop Jason, and he didn't kill Jesse, Scarlet, you, and me? It was all just a different universe?"

Her mind was a whirlwind of confusion and disbelief. She had vivid memories of the harrowing ordeal with Jason King, the daring plan to confront him, and the heart-pounding moments. But now, as she looked around her familiar Dallas facility, all of that felt like a distant dream.

Silas placed a comforting hand on her shoulder, his eyes filled with concern. "Amelia, it's a lot to process. I know," he said softly. "It'll take some time to adjust. What exactly happened?"

She explained how she had woken up in the machine. How

they cleaned up and went home. How they returned and discussed Jason's plans and how to take him down further. How Jason attempted to use The Vale Machine to go back in time to stop them, but it didn't work. How when they had arrived, they ended up dying.

As she recounted the events, she could see the weight of the situation sinking in for both Jesse and Silas. Their expressions shifted from confusion to comprehension to determination.

"So, it sounds like we aren't sure if Jason actually gained power and took over the world, but he was able to kill the three of us," Jesse said.

She nodded.

They went back through the story she had told them a few times to try and break everything down. From the sound of it, this world was *very* close to their own.

Amelia eventually needed to sit once more, mentally drained from recounting the complex events and from being in the machine for that long. "As much as I want to be here, I really want to go home and relax."

Jesse and Silas nodded.

"Yeah. Let's go home," Silas suggested.

"You two go home," Jesse said. "I'll finish up here and fill out the paperwork."

They thanked him, and Silas helped her into the car.

"Don't worry," he said. "I went home to let Lucy out and feed her."

As they drove back home, her mind was still racing with thoughts of the alternate reality. The events she had recounted felt so *real*, and the uncertainty of whether Jason King had truly gained power or if it was all a different world haunted her thoughts.

He glanced at her, sensing her inner turmoil. "Amelia, I know this is a lot to take in, but we are in this together. We will figure out the truth, and we will stop Jason."

She managed a weak smile. "Thanks, Silas. I don't know what I'd do without you and Jesse by my side."

Arriving home, they let Lucy out, and she couldn't help but feel a sense of comfort as she watched her puppy happily roam around the backyard. The world might be filled with uncertainty, but in that moment, there was a sense of normalcy that grounded her.

Silas fixed them some dinner as she sat in the living room. He brought it over for her, and they sat and ate. She scooted closer to him, trying to forget the pain she had witnessed. As they finished their meal, they sat in silence, the weight of their experiences hanging in the air.

Silas took it upon himself to clean the dishes, wanting to ease her burden as much as he could. Afterward, he helped her shower, where he lovingly washed away the physical and emotional residue of their recent trials. He selected a set of comfortable clothes for her to change into and gently assisted her into them. After guiding her back to the bed, he tucked her in, making sure she was warm and comfortable.

He then quickly took his own shower, dressed, and returned to the bed. After crawling under the covers, he pulled her close and held her tight, their bodies fitting together as if they were made for each other. In the quiet of their shared space, they talked, their voices low and filled with tenderness. He reminded her how much he loved her, his words soothing.

Amelia, still grappling with the shock of their discoveries, requested that he turn on the television. They found a channel broadcasting some lighthearted cartoons, and as they watched the colorful characters go on their comedic adventure, a sense of serenity settled over them. The laughter from the television filled the room, a welcome respite. Together, they held onto each other, finding solace in the simple joys of a quiet evening at home.

Eventually, exhaustion from their eventful day caught up with them, and their laughter gave way to drowsiness. Silas turned off the television, and they settled into a comfortable silence, content in each other's company.

The morning arrived, and Amelia woke to an empty bed. Yet Silas soon returned through the door.

She stretched and asked, "Where did you go, honey?"

He lifted a bag of donuts, tacos, and coffee. She smiled at the sight. She sat up, and he brought the food and drinks over to the bed and sat next to her. He kissed her. They soon sat there, eating and watching TV.

"I think we should get married," Amelia said.

Silas looked over at her, smiling. "I would love to, but where and with whom?"

She sat there, deep in thought. "Maybe we could do something small. Like go to the courthouse?"

"When would you like to? If you want, we could invite Jesse with his family, head down to South Padre tomorrow morning, and do it there."

She took a bite of a donut and pondered the idea. "Small and at the beach... I like it. We could get a hotel for the night. That would be fun."

They both beamed at the prospect.

The next morning, they called Jesse and shared the exciting news. He was absolutely thrilled for them. As they scoured the internet for hotels and an officiant, their excitement waned though. They couldn't find a marriage officiant who could accommodate their quick time line. Disappointment crept in.

Silas, never one to back down from a challenge, said, "What if we ask Jesse to do it? He could go online and register as an officiant."

Her eyes lit up, and she nodded enthusiastically. "I love that idea."

20

The Twentieth Chapter: Bells

The air felt lighter than it had in a long time. The sun shined its warmth, the birds sang their songs, and the bees danced from flower to flower.

As Silas and Amelia continued their car ride south, the landscape gradually transitioned from urban sprawl to open highways flanked by fields of wildflowers swaying in the breeze. The scent of the fresh air filled the car, carrying a sense of freedom and adventure. He occasionally reached over to hold her hand, their fingers interlocking. The road ahead seemed to stretch endlessly, but they welcomed the journey.

Eventually, they reached South Padre. He drove down a few streets, searching for their hotel. When he did, he gently shook her awake, her eyes fluttering open. She stretched, and her face beamed upon seeing their arrival.

While she got out and took Lucy to go to the bathroom, he ran inside to check in and grabbed a dolly to transport their suitcases and Lucy's bed to their room. As they loaded up the dolly, a vehicle pulled up behind them. They turned and saw Jesse with his family—Sandra and his daughter fast asleep in their car.

"I'll go ahead and park," Jesse said. "We'll go check in in a few and let you know when we're all done."

Amelia and Silas nodded and headed to their hotel room. Upon opening the door, they were impressed: two queen beds, a spacious shower with a rainfall showerhead, a Jacuzzi on the balcony, and a fridge stocked with snacks and drinks.

She noticed rose petals scattered all over the bed, forming the word *congrats*. She couldn't help but smile.

"Darn," Silas said, picking up a bottle of champagne. "That was supposed to be for tomorrow."

"Well, when have we ever done anything in any kind of order? I already have your last name," she quipped.

They both laughed and unloaded their suitcases. He fed Lucy while she finished putting away some of her stuff, including the dark blue dress she had picked out for the wedding. Once they were finished, he sent Jesse a text, letting him know they were done and suggesting seafood. Jesse replied with a thumbs-up and mentioned that they would head down in a few minutes.

"Do you want to grab a drink at the bar while we wait?" Silas asked.

Amelia nodded.

So, they headed down the elevator, found the bar, and both ordered their drinks. They then sipped them, taking in the atmosphere and the strangers all around them.

"Heyyy! There's the happy couple!"

They turned around and saw it was Jesse and his wife and daughter.

"Are you all ready for dinner?" Silas asked.

They all agreed. Silas and Amelia downed the rest of their drinks and left cash at the bar.

They all went to a fun seafood restaurant on a pier where the crashing of the waves and the chatter of people echoed throughout the restaurant. Laughter filled the air as they shared stories.

Jesse raised his glass for a toast. "I just wanted to say, with everything we've been through and everything to come, enjoy the moment. If you live the rest of your life like that, it'll be full of excitement and adventure. To the happy couple!"

They all cheered and laughed, thanking Jesse for the toast.

After many drinks and a hearty meal, they nearly closed the restaurant. Silas went to pay, but Jesse insisted on covering the bill. He and Amelia thanked them warmly. They gathered their things and left the restaurant, the adults slightly buzzed and in high spirits.

They walked back to the hotel, trading laughs and smart remarks. Once they arrived, Silas and Amelia found a couple of chairs at the bar. Jesse and Sandra went to put their daughter to sleep and joined them a few minutes later. They sat, drank, and relished each other's company, which they hadn't done in a long time. They drank well into the night, getting one more round of drinks once the last call was made. A few hours after the last call, they all headed to their rooms.

Silas and Amelia both collapsed onto their bed, full of booze and happiness.

She turned her head to look over at him, who barely had his eyes open. "I love you."

He smiled. "I love you too."

They tried stripping their clothes off but only managed to get their pants around their ankles and their shirts off. Not long after their attempt, they were both fast asleep. Between Lucy, Amelia, and Silas, there was no telling who was snoring.

They woke to banging coming from the door. Silas tried getting up, but the light outside was too bright, and he ended up rolling onto the floor. She groaned at the noise. He finally got to his feet and shuffled to the door, not remembering his pants were around his ankles. Only his boxers covered him. He cracked the door open with his eyes barely open.

"Morning, lovebirds," Jesse said. "I see y'all barely made it into pajamas. Here." He handed Silas two cups of coffee.

"Thanks," Silas said groggily.

"Meet us downstairs in like forty-five minutes for breakfast." He smiled. "Today is the big day!" He then walked off to his room.

Silas closed the door and shuffled back to the bed, sipping his coffee. Which started to bring him back to life. Which was when he realized what Jesse had meant. He looked down, noticed that he only had his boxers on, and laughed. "This isn't the worst thing he's seen me in."

He then gently spanked Amelia. "Time to get up, honey."

She groaned and pulled a pillow over her face.

He got out of bed and walked to the shower, turning it on. Afterward, he returned to the bed and removed their remaining clothes, his and hers. He struggled to get her out of bed but succeeded after several attempts. Once in the shower, the cold water felt like icicles running down their spines. She shivered.

After what felt like an eternity in the shower, they stepped out to dry. Amelia, still shivering from the cold, wrapped herself in several towels, and he hugged her to try and warm her up, which seemed to help. They walked over to the bed and both got dressed. He fed Lucy while she finished getting ready, and then they made their way down to the first floor for breakfast with Lucy in tow.

As the three of them walked into the dining area, Amelia took Lucy outside while Silas sat with Jesse and his family.

"How did y'all sleep?" Sandra asked with a wink.

"I don't even know. I remember falling onto the bed and then waking up from your husband knocking on the door. We had too much to drink..."

Jesse laughed. "Yeah, no shit. Oops. I mean, *poop*. No poop."

Sandra gave him a side-eye, but their daughter didn't seem to notice.

When Amelia got back, her and Silas went up to the breakfast buffet and grabbed some greasy bacon, eggs, and waffles. They also both snatched some juice and coffee and returned to the table to eat with Jesse and his family. Lucy lay beside them.

"So, what time do y'all want to get married?" Jesse asked with a mouthful of eggs.

Amelia swallowed her food. "Well, maybe before lunch. Then we can go get something to eat and sit by the beach all day."

They all agreed that it sounded like a great plan.

"Well, okay then," Sandra said as they finished eating. "Y'all go upstairs and then get dressed. Meet us down here at eleven a.m. on the dot. Shoo."

So, they did. They went up to their room, watched TV, and cuddled. Their hangover had worn off, but Amelia felt oddly nervous being next to him like this. Maybe it was the wedding. Or perhaps it was that she hadn't thought this would even happen a few months ago.

Before long, their alarm went off at 10:30 a.m. They quickly got dressed. He put on nice tan khaki pants, a button-down shirt, and flip-flops. She put her hair up and added a few flowers to her bun, including lavender, her favorite. She also put on a dress she had brought.

"Stunning, beautiful, gorgeous," Silas said, wrapping his arms around her from behind. "Those words don't even come close to how amazing you look."

She blushed. "Stop it. It was a last-minute idea."

He stuck out his arm, and they walked down to the elevator. When they exited, they saw Sandra waiting.

"Come with me," she said.

They followed her out the back of the hotel, down the stairs that led to the sand, and along the warm sand until they saw it—an arch adorned with white and red roses, lavender, bluebonnets, and daisies intertwined all around it.

"How beautiful! Did you do this all by yourself?" Amelia asked Sandra in awe.

Sandra shook her head. "No. I had some help from the little one and Jesse. We worked on it last night and this morning. That's why we were a little behind yesterday. We had to pick it up."

Tears formed in Amelia's eyes. She had never seen anything quite as beautiful.

As she and Silas walked toward the arch, they noticed two chairs for Sandra and their daughter, both placed in the middle. Sandra sat next to her daughter, and they joined Jesse at the front.

"You both look stunning." Jesse smiled at them. "Let's get the show started."

The ceremony was simple and easy yet beautiful. The seagulls chatted away, the waves crashed along the shore, and the many onlookers watched in silence.

"Do you two have any vows you want to say?" Jesse asked.

They both looked at each other; they hadn't thought about this.

"I...I won't make any promises because they can easily be broken," Silas said after a moment, "and I'm not one to break promises. But there is one thing I will say: I will never leave you again. You are stuck with me forever. That is a promise that won't be broken."

Amelia teared up. "Well, now you took what I was going to say."

They all softly laughed.

"You're right though. Making promises is a mistake. Besides this one—you won't lose me either. But if I do lose you, even if it's at the grocery store, I will always come for you. There is nothing in this world that will stop me from doing that, Silas Vale."

They both smiled, exchanged rings, and kissed.

Cheers erupted from all around, not just from the small group but also from the onlookers. They waved to the crowd that had gathered.

"Who's ready for lunch, margaritas, and sitting on the beach?" Jesse said.

21

The Twenty First Chapter: Moments

Upstairs, Silas and Amelia grabbed their swimsuits with him keeping his button-down shirt on.

Before she could put on her swimsuit and cover though, he said, "Stop." He sat there, admiring her body in all its beauty.

She blushed, walked over to him, and kissed him. He placed his hands on her hips, which made her arm hairs stand on end.

"We need to head down, husband," she said, smiling.

He smiled back at her. "Wife, I never thought before meeting you I would be saying that word to you."

She kissed him again, slid her bathing suit on, and threw on her cover-up. They headed downstairs with Lucy and their beach equipment. There, they met Jesse and his family.

"We had an idea," Jesse said. "What if you ladies go find a spot, and us two guys will go pick up food and bring it back. We can then eat and chill on the beach."

Silas and Amelia agreed.

The ladies walked down to the beach with Lucy, while Silas and Jesse went to grab sandwiches from a local sandwich shop.

As they waited in line at the shop, Jesse asked, "So, how does it feel, Mr. Married Man?"

Silas laughed and shrugged. "Honestly, it feels like it did yesterday but better, I guess. I'm just happy it's finally happened."

"I'm glad as well. Even before you two got together, I knew it would happen. My only advice is to not go to bed angry, and at least once a week, make a night for just the two of you. And try to travel. Enjoy each other and make memories whenever you can."

He nodded and thanked him.

They placed their orders at the counter and walked over to the side.

"We have a lot to do with this whole Jason thing once we get back, don't we?" Silas said. "We should probably link up with Scarlet."

Jesse stood there, contemplating. "We do, but don't you worry about that today. Let's go enjoy our time away with our wives."

He agreed, pushing aside his thoughts of what was to come.

The two friends collected their sandwiches and returned to the beach, where they found the ladies seated on a colorful beach towel with Lucy playing in the sand nearby. The sun hung high in the sky, casting an inviting glow over the sparkling water and golden sands.

They all dug into their sandwiches, savoring the taste. As they enjoyed their meal, their conversation turned to lighthearted topics, such as their favorite vacation spots and childhood memories. Lucy, their ever-energetic companion, chased seagulls and dug holes in the sand, eliciting laughter from the group.

After satisfying their hunger, they reclined on their beach towels, basking in the sun's warmth. The discussion shifted to plans for the remainder of the day, and they decided to take a stroll along the shore, collecting seashells and building sandcastles.

Walking hand in hand with Amelia, Silas couldn't help but think that this was the perfect way to commence their new life together—good friends, beautiful scenery, and hope for the future.

"I couldn't have asked for a better way to celebrate our wedding," Amelia said.

He nodded with a smile. "I agree. This has been the best day of my life."

As they walked down the beach, she found a few silver dollar shells. They talked about their future together, collecting shells until their hands were full and until his swim trunks couldn't hold any more. Eventually, they made their way back to Jesse and his family.

Sandra was watching their daughter while Jesse was asleep. Silas and Amelia joined Sandra's daughter in making a sand-castle, adding the seashells they had found to the structure. The little girl was thrilled they had joined her. Her lively spirit and vivid imagination took them on a journey, where seagulls transformed into dragons and dolls became princesses and knights who battled the fearsome dragons.

The soothing sound of the waves and the joyous laughter of the girl made it feel like time had slowed just for them.

After they completed their sandcastle masterpiece, they all sat back to admire their creation. Beaming, Jesse's daughter thanked them both for helping create the best castle she had ever seen. Jesse, who had woken up during their sandcastle building, playfully scooped up his daughter. She squealed and laughed as he carried her into the ocean. Silas, Sandra, and

Amelia all laughed at the sight.

Amelia sat next to the sandcastle, gazing at the ocean and letting the sun warm her skin. Silas got up and walked over to the ice chest next to Sandra. He reached in and grabbed two mixed drinks.

"You two are adorable. I'm so happy that you and Amelia are together," Sandra said.

Silas grinned, but his smile wavered. "I am too, but I'm worried that Jason could use our relationship against us."

She removed her sunglasses and looked him in the eyes. "Don't let that seed of fear take root in you. If you do, you'll be constantly looking over your shoulder and worrying. Nothing bad will happen, Silas. Go and love your wife." She ended her words with a warm smile.

He nodded appreciatively. Her wisdom had always been a source of comfort to him.

He opened one of the drinks and handed it to her before returning to Amelia, who was still lost in thought by the sandcastle. As he approached her, the sea breeze mixed with their drinks' tropical aroma created a tranquil atmosphere. He handed her a drink and sat beside her.

He leaned in and gently kissed her, the taste of their mixed drinks adding a sweet note to the moment. They sat there side by side—their love stronger than any fear that might try to creep in.

Silas stared at her and gave a grin.

She became nervous. "W-what?"

He stood, grabbed her arm, flipped her onto his shoulder, and ran toward the water.

"No! No! No! No!" she screamed, laughing.

They crashed into an incoming wave, and both went under.

When she jumped up, she laughed and said, "I hate you, Silas!"

However, she didn't see him.

She looked all over until a hand grabbed her ankle, causing her to jump. He came out of the water, giggling. She glared at him but smiled and splashed him with water.

Their playful water fight continued, their laughter and splashing turning the beach into their own private playground. The sun hung low on the horizon, casting a warm, golden glow across the sand and the sea.

As the day wore on, they built sandcastles together, each one more elaborate than the last. He, with his creative touch, sculpted intricate turrets and bridges, while she added seashells and colorful pebbles as embellishments.

When the evening approached, they found themselves sitting side by side again, watching the sun's descent into the water. The sky painted shades of orange and pink, and the waves whispered secrets of the sea.

Sandra and Jesse slowly walked up to them.

"We want you two to go have a nice dinner alone, a date night," Sandra said, handing Silas and Amelia an envelope filled with a few hundred dollars in cash. "We will see you all in the morning before heading out."

Amelia glanced inside the envelope and held it back out. "No, we can't take this."

Jesse pushed the envelope back. "We want you to have it. It's your wedding day after all. It isn't much, but go treat yourselves. And let us know when you get back, so we know you're safe. We will also watch Lucy. Just leave a key at the front desk so we can get her food and bed."

Amelia and Silas glanced at each other and thanked Jesse and

Sandra several times, but they shooed them off.

They soon headed back to their hotel room to get changed. She quickly changed into a beautiful dress she had packed for the occasion, while he opted for a sharp suit that had been hanging in the closet.

He looked at her with a mischievous grin. "Where should we go for our date night? Any particular place you've been craving?"

She pondered this for a moment, her eyes sparkling. "How about that charming little Italian restaurant we passed earlier today? It looked so romantic, and I've been craving pasta."

He nodded, his heart dancing. "Perfect choice. Let's make it a night to remember."

As they left, they placed the envelope of cash in his pocket, grateful for the support of their friends. They walked out of the hotel and strolled down the street. He had her arm wrapped around his. She rested her head on his shoulder as they walked.

After about a quarter of a mile, they arrived at the restaurant and were promptly seated. The waitress brought over a nice bottle of wine and appetizers. They savored their meal, enjoying each other's company and observing the other patrons at the restaurant. They created humorous stories about random people, speculating their conversations and professions.

Their laughter filled the cozy ambiance, blending with the soft murmur of conversations and the gentle clinking of silverware. As the evening wore on, they exchanged loving glances and subtle touches.

The night was filled with magic.

As they finished their meals, the waitress walked over with a tray of desserts and a bottle of champagne. "A nice gentleman called in, saying he was your friend and that you both had just gotten married. He wanted to send this over to you." She set a chocolate cake, the bottle of champagne, glasses for the champagne, and gelato on their table.

"Oh my goodness, thank you," Amelia said. She looked at Silas, her face flushed from the wine. "We will have to thank Jesse and Sandra when we see them tomorrow."

He nodded.

They dug into the wonderful dessert and sipped their champagne, savoring every bite. They couldn't help but steal glances at each other, their love illuminated by the soft candlelight. With the last bite of cake and the final sip of champagne, they toasted to their new life together.

Smiling, they paid the bill and left, their hearts full of gratitude. The night was still young, so they walked along the beach, shoes in hand. The water washed over their feet as they held hands. They didn't say much, just little jokes and small giggles. Silas looked over at her, who was shining in the moonlight. Her beauty was heightened by the moon's gentle glow. He dropped his shoes, grabbed her waist, and pulled her in close.

She tasted like chocolate and champagne. She relaxed into him, drawing him nearer, and he could feel her heartbeat through their clothing. They held that kiss for what felt like a lifetime—a lifetime they never wanted to end.

As they finally broke the kiss, their breaths mingled with the cool ocean breeze. The crashing waves provided a soothing backdrop. They gazed into each other's eyes, their love speaking volumes in the silence.

As they slowly walked hand in hand once more, their laughter and their love filled the night.

22

The Twenty Second Chapter:Message

The next morning, Amelia and Silas woke up, feeling refreshed and reluctant to let go of each other. They knew they would eventually need to get up and go get breakfast. However, they held each other a bit longer, savoring each other's warmth with their legs intertwined. Her chest pressed against his side, her arms wrapped around him.

In that intimate embrace, time seemed to stand still. The soft light filtering through the curtains painted their entwined bodies with a warm, golden glow.

He gently kissed the top of her head. "Breakfast can wait a little longer," he whispered, his voice full of warmth.

She responded with a soft, contented sigh and nuzzled closer to him.

In that moment, they relished the simple joy of being together, basking in the comfort they found in each other's arms.

Eventually, they got dressed and headed down to the first floor for breakfast, where they found Jesse.

"Hey, you two," he said. "How was it?"

Smiling, they both looked at each other. She blushed. They

quickly told him about dinner and thanked him for the desert.

He looked at them, confused. "I didn't send y'all anything."

"What do you mean?" she asked. "The waitress said you sent us cake and champagne."

"No? We ordered pizza and watched a movie last night."

"Well...who did that then?" Silas asked.

They all stared at one another, trying to figure it out. But they soon decided to put it aside for the moment and enjoy breakfast. Silas and Amelia made themselves a meal and sat with Jesse.

"Where is the rest of your family?" Amelia asked.

"Upstairs," Jesse said. "They're getting dressed to come down. I had been up for a while and just came down early to get coffee."

Sandra and their daughter showed up as soon as he finished his sentence. Sandra gave Silas and Amelia the same look he had, asking how it was last night. They both told her about how wonderful dinner was. Amelia asked her if she was the one who had ordered the cake and champagne, to which she shook her head.

"Could it have been a mix-up at the restaurant?" Jesse asked. "Maybe they delivered it to the wrong table."

"Yeah..." Amelia said. "Maybe it was a mix-up. Who knows?"

"But we do have a long drive ahead of us, so maybe we should take off soon."

They all agreed, continuing to eat their breakfast. Sandra let Amelia know that Lucy was very well-behaved, which made Amelia happy. They finished up their breakfast not long after.

They all quickly finished packing. Downstairs, they all met up, along with Lucy, whose tail was wagging to see his owners. They then checked out of the hotel and walked out to their cars.

"Let me know when y'all get home," Silas said.

Jesse nodded.

"Thank you both again," Amelia said.

Sandra hugged them both. Jesse did the same.

Silas and Amelia got in their car with Lucy in the back seat. And off they went back on the road to Dallas.

The miles stretched out before them, the mystery from earlier fading into the background. The car's stereo played a mix of their favorite songs. Lucy settled in the back seat, alternating between napping and pressing her snout against the window to take in the passing scenery.

Silas and Amelia chatted about their trip and reminisced about the great time they had spent with Jesse and his family. The miles melted away as they recounted their adventures and talked about their plans for the upcoming weeks.

About halfway through the journey, they stopped for a quick lunch at a cozy roadside diner. Lucy happily joined them, and the friendly waitress even brought her a bowl of water. They enjoyed some delicious food before hitting the road again.

As they continued their drive, their conversation shifted to more serious matters. They discussed their work, their dreams for the future, and even some challenges they faced. It was these heart-to-heart conversations that grew their bond even stronger.

As the sun began to dip below the horizon, Silas, Amelia, and Lucy arrived in Dallas. They let Jesse know they had arrived home, and he did the same. Lucy hopped out, running to the front yard as she had been holding it for most of the drive home. Inside, they dumped their laundry from the trip into the washer and sat on the couch to decompress.

Even though it was the same home they had lived in before, it felt new to them now as a married couple.

During their enjoyment, they both received text messages in a group chat with Jesse from a number they did not recognize. The images the texts contained included shots of them at their wedding, featuring Jesse's family, Amelia and Silas at dinner, Silas and Amelia in the ocean, and Jesse and his daughter in the ocean.

They looked at each other.

"Who sent us these?" Amelia asked.

He shrugged. "I don't know. We didn't take them."

Another text message came in. "Hello, you three. It's been a few minutes, huh? Well, I'm sure you are wondering who the hell took these. To answer your question, I did not, but it's fun what you can do with a little extra cash and a desperate person. But don't worry. I'm not here to hurt you. In reality, I don't want to see you three. I won't be bothering you all for now, so continue your lives without me. See you around. Jason."

Amelia dropped her phone. "*See you around?* Has he been *watching* us this whole time? Is this a threat, Silas?"

He sat there, rereading the message and trying to understand what exactly it meant. "I don't know. I don't think he means anything by it, other than exactly what he said."

His phone lit up with a call from Jesse. He answered and put it on speakerphone.

"Did you see the text?" Jesse asked.

"Yes," they both said.

"What could it mean?" he asked

Silas spoke up, telling him what he had just explained to Amelia.

"I think you might be right, but we can't be too careful. If he wanted us dead, he would have killed us already, right?"

They sat there in silence for a few minutes.

"I don't think he wants to do anything to us, but how do we know he isn't trying to create the machine again?" Silas said.

Amelia laughed out of nervousness. "We don't know. That's the scary part."

"So, what do we do?"

"I believe we need to sleep on it and go into the office tomorrow to talk," Jesse said. "There is nothing we can do now, so let's not worry or stress about it."

Silas and Amelia hesitated but agreed. The phone call disconnected.

"I can't believe he was watching us…" she said.

"I believe it," Silas said. "He told us before that he had the resources to always know where we were. I think Jesse is right. We will talk more about it tomorrow. Let's just enjoy our evening together now."

With their decision made, they tried to put the unsettling message behind them for the rest of the evening. They decided to make dinner. It was like a dance from cutting the vegetables to the frying pan. They worked so well together that they never even bumped into each other. Lucy was fed and let outside to go the bathroom. Silas placed the plates on the table.

"Oh!" Amelia said, remembering a surprise she had planned. "There was one thing I forgot to bring with me that could help relax us." She practically skipped to the bedroom.

Silas stood there, confused. She then came out wearing nothing but a lace dark blue lingerie, exposing nearly every part of her fair smooth skin. His jaw dropped.

"Well, I guess we better eat quickly," he said, smiling.

Clothes fell to the floor, bodies pressed against each other as they became one. In the dimly lit room, their love was a fiery dance of passion and longing. The world outside faded away as they lost themselves in the ecstasy of their union. Each touch—each kiss—was a declaration of their love, a testament to the bond they shared.

They moved from the kitchen into their bedroom to continue their exploration of one another. They found satisfaction multiple times until they were both beyond content.

Afterward, they recalled that Lucy had been left outside, so Silas decided to go let her in. When he returned, she was in the shower with water flowing down her perfect body. He couldn't resist the enticing sight before him. He joined her, the warm water enveloping them as their bodies pressed close once more. The intimate connection between them was as powerful as ever, and the water's gentle caress seemed to heighten their senses.

His hands caressed every inch of her body, reveling in the sensation of every curve and contour. By the time he was done, she was left with weak legs and a radiant smile. In return, she explored his body with the same sensual attention, igniting his desire in kind.

After they had washed away the remnants of their evening and dried off, they shared a tender kiss before slipping into their comfortable bed, the warmth of their connection providing solace and security as they drifted off into a contented sleep.

23

The Twenty Third Chapter: Continue

The sound of a computer closing signaled a man's entrance into the dimly lit room. Shadows danced across the walls, mirroring the uncertainty that hung in the air.

"So, what are you going to do?" Joel asked.

There was a sigh in the darkness, followed by the screeching of a chair on a wooden floor and footsteps. Emerging from the darkness was Jason.

"Let's leave them alone for now," Jason said. "We have our own plans we need to do. We're nearly done with that other machine they didn't want us to have, but if I threaten them now, they'll want to look more into what I'm doing. And we need them off our backs."

Joel nodded.

"Have you found my family?"

"Yes, sir. I was just coming to tell you this."

Jason cleared his throat. "Good. We'll leave in the morning."

Joel nodded and left the room.

Jason walked into the living room, poured himself a scotch, and sat there deep in thought—staring at a television that was not on. He contemplated the complex web of alliances and rivalries that had brought him to this point. With a heavy sigh, he knew he had to wait a little longer for the power he so heavily pursued. But as long as he can get those three off his back, he might have a chance.

Outside, rain rhythmically tapped against the windowpane, providing a soothing backdrop to his contemplations. It was also a reminder that even in the midst of uncertainty, life continued to move forward.

As the night deepened, his thoughts grew more intricate. He envisioned the intricate dance of power and strategy that lay ahead. Using the room's shadows, he found the determination to forge a path through the labyrinthine challenges that awaited him.

Jason emptied his scotch and continued to ponder but not too much. He didn't want his paranoia to get the best of him. Before long, the planning and thinking had him drifting off to sleep.

A crash stirred Jason, and he looked around to find that the glass he had been holding had fallen onto the floor and shattered. He wiped his eyes, cleaned up the glass, and got ready for the day—opting for his customary suit. He had to make this reunion count.

He had to steal his family back.

With his packed bag zipped up and ready, he glanced at the clock, realizing that the hour was approaching. He'd soon need to embark on the journey to reclaim his loved ones. As he lay on the bed, fatigue and anticipation mingled within him. He knew the challenges ahead would test him in ways he could scarcely imagine. Closing his eyes, he hoped for a few moments of respite before the storm that awaited him.

He awoke to a text from Joel that indicated he would arrive in thirty minutes. He poured himself a cup of coffee, sipping it slowly. The flight ahead to Spain would be long, but he was fortunate enough to have access to a private plane for the journey.

Finishing his coffee, he placed the empty cup in the sink and headed toward the door. Just as he opened it, he found Joel standing there, ready to knock. "Ready?"

Joel nodded. "We have someone watching their house to ensure that if they leave, we'll know where they are."

"Good."

With Joel as his companion, he made his way to the waiting vehicle, climbed inside, and set off for the airport.

As Jason and Joel traversed through the historic streets and highways of Spain, they made their way toward the house where Jason's family was located.

"They should still be at the house," Joel remarked. However, he couldn't help but ask one question. "Why would you want to bring them back after what happened?"

Jason sat in contemplation, staring out the window as the scenery passed by. "Because I need them," he said with a determined tone. "I need to maintain my image with the people, and when I gain control, they need to be with me. But if they disagree, I'll proceed without them. They are just tools for the future."

After about half an hour, they arrived at a small villa.

Jason sat there, gazing at the villa. "Well, it's time." He exited the vehicle, walked up to the house, and took a deep breath before knocking on the door.

He could hear the girls laughing and playing inside, a sound that briefly stirred a small part of his former self. But he suppressed it, resolute in his determination to avoid returning to the person he once was—someone he considered weak.

As he waited, footsteps approached the door. It unlocked and opened slightly, revealing Sarah.

"Hello?" she said cautiously from behind the door.

"Hey, Sarah," he said with a mixture of hope and apprehension. "It's me. It's time to come home."

The door opened further, and Sarah stood there, though her demeanor did not seem welcoming. Instead, her face bore a fearful, concerned expression, and her body blocked the entrance. In a stern, whispered voice, she asked, "What are you doing here? I made myself clear. We don't want anything to do with you."

"I understand," Jason replied. "But I need you three to come home. I have big plans. Plans to regain power—more power than I had before. And I need you all to make it happen."

In the background, the girls continued to play, their cheerful voices oblivious to the weighty conversation taking place at the door.

Sarah glanced back inside and then stepped out. "I will be right here, girls. You keep playing." She closed the door behind her, creating some distance between them. Her cold stare then turned back on him. "You *shot* our eldest!"

He feigned a somber expression. "I know I wasn't thinking. But I want you all back, and I'm willing to get Scarlet back as well."

She remained unconvinced, her voice laced with suspicion and resentment. "No, you won't, and no, you don't feel bad. You hated her from day one, and I will never understand why."

This brought irritation to Jason. "Don't tell me how I feel, you…" He stopped himself, but the frustration was evident.

Sarah laughed. "No. Go ahead. Say it. Call me what you think. You believe I'm some fool who will do whatever you say, but that isn't true. I left because you're dangerous, not just to me but to my daughters. You are the problem, Jason. Not Scarlet. Not anyone else. You."

His face contorted. "I'm the problem? *I'm* the problem?" His tone edged with anger. "Ha! I'm not the problem. I'm the *solution*. You're just too dense to see that. You and all those who oppose me."

Their argument hung in the air like a thick fog, charged with tension and unresolved grievances. Her unwavering resolve clashed with his unyielding determination, and it seemed neither was willing to back down.

Amid the heated exchange, laughter and playful voices from the two girls playing inside the house continued to serve as a stark reminder of the fragile situation at hand. Innocent bystanders caught in the crossfire of their parents' turbulent relationship.

Sarah took a step closer to him, her eyes locked onto his. "You don't understand, Jason. Power has consumed you. You've become someone we don't recognize anymore."

His anger intensified, yet he couldn't deny that her words had struck a chord. "I'm not the problem. And I'm not consumed by power. I *control* the power. It lives within me, and I use it to my advantage. You'll see." He sighed. "I planned to at least see the girls, but that's obviously not going to happen. Besides, I'm better off without you or them. I don't need any of you."

Sarah looked at him, fierce determination in her eyes. "If that's how you feel, then go. Go and abuse your power. But mark my words, it will be your downfall. You will fall harder than a falling oak tree. You *will* fall. And there won't be a single thing you can do about it."

He laughed. "*I* will fall? Please don't make me laugh. I will not fail."

Sandra looked down on him. "Go," she commanded, her voice firm and unyielding. "Whatever your motives may be, it's time for you to leave. You don't belong here." She pointed at Joel and the two vehicles parked on the street. "And take your dogs with you."

24

The Twenty Fourth Chapter: Where am I?

The sun rose, bringing a new day and a fresh start to Silas and Amelia's life together.

He stretched and looked down, her still wrapped around him. He lifted the bedsheet and admired her beautiful body. She was like a work of art to him, a masterpiece that was his and no one else's. Smiling, he slowly unhooked her legs and her arms from around him.

She didn't stir.

He stood and stretched before quietly walking out of the bedroom. He let their dog out into the backyard. In the kitchen, he filled Lucy's bowl and contemplated what to make for Amelia. After scanning through the food, he decided on pancakes, bacon, and eggs. As he finished up, footsteps approached.

"No clothes, huh? I like your butt." Amelia wrapped her arms around him, pressing her bare skin against his back.

"I guess you had the same idea."

They both smiled.

She kissed his cheek, grabbed a piece of bacon, and took a bite before walking over to the table to sit. He brought her a plate of pancakes, bacon, and eggs, along with a cup of coffee. Excited, she even did a little dance that made him laugh. He brought his own plate to the table and sat across from her. As they ate, they talked about their favorite parts of the night before, and her feet kept playing with his.

Afterward, they cleaned the dishes and prepared for the day ahead. They then walked out of the house, leaving Lucy behind, and set off for the facility, ready to confront the uncertainties that lay ahead.

They only stopped once for coffee for them and Jesse. Upon their arrival, they both felt delighted to see the facility again. They entered the building and noticed the hustle and bustle had just begun as people started arriving. They walked down the hallways and toward the office they had agreed to meet at. When they entered, Jesse was already sitting in a chair, examining the machine and the data with a box of donuts on the table. They exchanged greetings, and Silas handed him his cup of coffee.

"I texted Scarlet," Jesse said. "She will give us a call in a few minutes to discuss everything."

They both nodded and sat to review the text message they had received from Jason. When the time came, Jesse's phone rang, and he answered it, putting it on speaker.

"Hey, Scarlet," he said. "It's Jesse, Amelia, and Silas. You're on speakerphone."

Scarlet greeted them, and they responded in kind. She shared updates she had received on Jason's movements, including his place of residence and his plans to leave the country, presumably to reunite with his family. They were shocked by this news. After she finished her updates, she inquired about the text message. Jesse sent her a screenshot of it.

"So, he doesn't want anything to do with you all?" she asked.

"That's what he said, but I'm having a hard time believing this," he said.

"Well, honestly, we don't know for sure. What we can do is keep an eye on him. You all should continue with your plans, and I'll keep you updated."

"Maybe..." Amelia said. "I don't know. I just don't trust him. I mean, who would?"

"You're right. We can't fully trust him. But we can't sit here and worry about him 24-7 either."

They sat there for a moment, pondering this.

"Well, what's the worst thing he can do that we haven't already assumed or thought he would do?" Silas said. "Scarlet, are you sure you have a tight crew watching him?"

There were a few seconds of silence.

"Yes," she said. "I personally go check on them. And to figure out what country he may be escaping to, we're planning to get someone on the inside, either by recruiting them or putting them on the inside."

As the conversation continued, a sense of determination settled among them. They knew they had to remain vigilant and be prepared for any scenario. Scarlet's assurance about her team's surveillance offered a glimmer of hope, but the uncertainty surrounding Jason's intentions still weighed on their minds.

"All right, Scarlet," Jesse said. "Keep us updated on any developments. In the meantime, we will stay cautious and focused on our work, including exploring other universes in search of an answer to stop him."

With a plan in place, they ended the call, ready to embark on their new mission with renewed determination.

"We will have to fight him eventually," Silas said. "There is no other choice when it comes down to it."

"Let's not worry about what's to come but appreciate what we have now, which is each other and our work," Amelia said. "We may not have chosen this fight, but we have to be ready when it finds us."

He reached out, taking her hand in a reassuring grip. "You're right. We must be prepared, but we shouldn't let that be our sole focus. We've faced incredible challenges together, and we've always found a way through. This will be no different."

"Yes," Jesse added, adding his hand into the mix. "In the meantime, let's keep searching. Who knows? We might stumble upon something that can help us stop him."

As they stood there, their hands joined in solidarity, they knew the road ahead would be rough and uncertain. However, they took comfort in the fact they would face the dangers together.

They outlined their plans and established a schedule that balanced their responsibilities with The Echo Machine exploration. They even scheduled meetings with their employees to engage with new clients, providing only vague information about working on a new project. As the day drew to a close, they each went their separate ways.

For the rest of the week, they adhered to their schedule. Their days were filled with a mixture of client meetings and intense exploration of other universes. As they delved deeper into their research, they encountered countless variations of reality, each offering unique insights and challenges. Some universes held technological advancements beyond their wildest dreams, while others presented civilizations facing dire consequences. The diversity of worlds they explored was both awe-inspiring and humbling.

Monday arrived, and they settled into their daily routine. On this particular morning, it was Amelia's turn to go in the machine. They set everything up and plugged her in, their actions so routine like muscle memory.

"Ready for E-0087?" Silas asked as he powered on the machine.

She nodded, and Jesse initiated the countdown. She took a few deep breaths, mentally preparing herself. The room filled with the machine's rhythmic tapping and colorful flashing lights. She then slipped into unconsciousness.

The world around her transformed into a vast field, where she stood in the middle. To her surprise, she was dressed in metal shoulder plates, leather arm bands, a dark leather breastplate, and a hood. Her eyes drifted around her eerie, foreboding surroundings.

A terrifying noise reverberated through the air—a deep, thunderous roar that sounded like the sky was being ripped apart in the distance. The sound echoed, and the clouds overhead grew dark, obscuring the sun. Her heart raced as an eerie stillness settled over the landscape.

Even the tall grass around her ceased to sway.

From above, another screech pierced the air. A sense of impending doom loomed over her. Finally, the source of the commotion revealed itself—a colossal dragon with golden and dark blue scales.

It soared through the sky, its body stretching as long as a tower. Each of its wings could have spanned an entire football field. The dragon passed overhead, casting a shadow over her. She crouched in the tall grass to hide, her heart pounding.

The temperature dropped twenty degrees in a span of a blink.

"Amelia!" a voice yelled from the distant tree line.

Her head swiveled, looking for who said her name. Off to her left, a figure hid most of their body behind a thick tree. Their hand waved at her to follow.

"Hurry!" the voice said. "Run!"

Afterword

The story continues in **The Silent Machine.** Thank you for diving into Book 2 of the Vale Trilogy! Be on the lookout for more to come. I am currently working on several other books, including **Aetheria**, a post-apocalyptic story, and **The Cons-Piracy**, which tells the tale of a man who falls down the rabbit hole, among many others.

About the Author

From his beginnings in Owatonna, Minnesota, to finding his home in the landscapes of Oklahoma and Texas, particularly the vibrant city of San Antonio, Austin Brower's journey has been one of growth and discovery. Following eight years of service in the Texas Army National Guard, including a deployment to Somalia, Austin embarked on a new chapter in higher education and unexpectedly discovered a passion for writing. As a novice storyteller with a love for fantasy and science fiction, Austin is eager to hone his craft and share his unique voice with the world.

You can connect with me on:
- https://linktr.ee/AustinBrowerAuthor
- https://www.facebook.com/profile.php?id=61555386538355
- https://battleboundbranding.com

Also by Austin Brower

The Vale Machine

Uncover the secret that could rewrite history and forge the future in the heart of Texas. Silas, Amelia, and Jesse labor relentlessly within an unassuming facility, their dedication centered on The Machine— a revolutionary time travel device designed to break the barriers of time itself. As they delve deeper into its capabilities, they confront a formidable adversary: an enigmatic president who views The Machine not as a means of healing, but as a powerful tool to reshape destinies. With the president's ambitions as vast as the cosmos, they find themselves entangled in a web of intrigue and danger, where the fate of humanity hangs in the balance.

www.ingramcontent.com/pod-product-compliance
Lightning Source LLC
Chambersburg PA
CBHW060324310726
48976CB00007B/2439